The Death of the Dragon Keepers

by

Risaria

'You must keep quiet, or they will kill you too, my darling, and you have to live for all our sakes...for you have to bring the dragons back.'

In the only Kingdom left on earth an innocent child is born to be the last dragonkeeper – to somehow bring dragons and magic back to the world. But how?

Risaria is a storyteller, film-maker and workshop leader.
www.risaria.co.uk

2

First published 2014 in the UK by fruitful voices 151 Sidney Grove Newcastle NE4 5PE UK

Cover Art: Eye of the Dragon Cas Holmes www.casholmestextiles.co. uk

To my parents Norman and Geordie Mary for hatching and rearing me so beautifully.

The Death of the Dragon Keepers.

Chapters

The School

'The School' – I remember 'The School'.

I remember because it was my last contact with anyone in the outside world – eight years ago. The memory helps me realise that I'm not missing anything; it reinforces my desire to stay in my rooftop hideaway. Whenever I begin to hanker for more: more freedom, more space, or to walk outside, in the streets, the Forest – I'm not even sure I remember the Forest for real, or if the Forest is the one from my imagination, from the stories my Granpa used to read me – then I remind

myself of 'The Last Day'. I
call it 'The Last Day' because
it was the end of life as I knew
it.
It was also the last day
that I went to school:

'Azra!'
Startled, I look up; the
whole class is staring at me.
How long has the teacher been
calling my name?

I can't start at the
beginning; I don't remember it,
at any rate only flashes of it,
like seeing it out of the corner
of my eye. So my first memory
of that day is sitting at a desk –
I am eight years old and my
mother has dyed my hair to fit
in amid the sea of brown/black
heads of the Settlers. My skin
can pass for a Settler. My father
was a Settler with a good mix
of Arab in his blood and that
helps me in the great heat of

9

this desert land but my red hair marks me out as a Mackenzie – even though it's three hundred years since my ancestors flew here with the first flight of Caledonian dragons, a wedding gift uniting the people of Set with the Scots. Legend has it that my great-great-grandfather – I don't know how many greats but so many that even Granpa Jonas wasn't sure – came with these two dragons, a mother and daughter, when Sheikh Adam declared that the land of Set was a kingdom and he was the first king. The Sheikh's daughter was marrying the son of his old university friend, Dougal Mackenzie, Laird of Lanarkshire. Back then, dragons were revered and symbols of good luck and authority. What had gone wrong in those three hundred years I don't know. I just know that everything changed with the Dragon Wars and now everyone hates dragons, everyone except for my mum and me.

Until that day, I didn't know why, but my mother had done her best to try to protect me and help me to fit in: dyed my hair, dressed me in the clothes the others wore, passed me off as a boy, but it made no odds – no matter how hard I tried, I was different from the others.

That was the moment I woke up – in school, sitting at that island of a desk, surrounded by all the others. They're chatting, laughing, joking, fighting – but for me they were just wallpaper, a background hum. I sit there, yet I'm not there. Then, *whump*, there's a thud as Mr Simpson

slams his ruler down on my
desk.

'Azra!'

He is eye to eye with me.

'Ah! At last! We have
contact. Good of you to join us.
Now Azra, when was the last
dragon slain? And I will give
you a clue.'

He steps up to the easel
and unveils a picture that makes
us all gasp. I've heard of the
old arts, painting on glass, and
there are even stories of glass
boxes with moving pictures but
these are tales of olden times
and mainly traveller's tales.
What takes my breath away is
the way the sunlight hits the
glass and the colours explode
into the room. There's a knight
in leather armour and it must be
our King – a bit obvious
because he's wearing a crown –
with one foot on the serpentine,
scaly neck of the dragon.

Mr Simpson is still asking questions.

'Anyone know the answer?

A boy is jumping up and down, 'I know, I know, sir.'

'All right, Roland, what is the answer?'

'Five years ago, sir, when Prince Sam was three... I know that, sir, cos I was born the same moon as Prince Sam. And that's him in the picture too, sir. That's our Prince Sam.'

'Prince Samardashee,' Mr Simpson corrects him.

The picture shows the boy-prince wearing a coronet and holding a tiny, but lethal, sword. His face is smeared with red stripes. Mr Simpson points to the stripes. 'And who knows what this is?'

Roland is now reaching his arm so high to the ceiling the strain shows in his face. 'Sir!'

'All right, Roland, tell us.'

'It's dragon's blood, sir. Prince Sam was blooded with the dragon's blood cos he killed it, even though he was only *three*, sir!'

'Well, yes, he delivered the fatal blow,' Mr Simpson qualifies the remark.

We all know this story but the blood-bright picture brings it to life and the three boys next to me start whispering about how they would have killed the dragon. The girl behind me says, 'He's so brave, I mean my little brother's only three, he couldn't have done that.'

I can't help it, I start to cry. Tears are streaming down my face and all the other kids are looking at me, horrified. One boy calls out, 'Sir, he's crying, sir.'

'There's no need for that, boy, just because you don't know the answer.'

By now I'm not crying, I'm sobbing and, in trying to stop myself, I start hiccupping so it takes a long time to get out, 'That's...not...why ... I'm...crying.'

'Then what is it?'

'It's so beautiful!'

Mr Simpson is surprised. He looks again at the painting. 'I suppose it is beautiful, Azra, our Prince in such a heroic pose.'

But it's not the prince that I am looking at. 'Not the prince, sir, it's the dragon – it's so beautiful.'

I knew everyone hated dragons, my mother had told me, but now I *knew* – if you get what I mean. I could feel the emotion, the shock-horror travelling around the room. A girl at the front turns around in her seat and, as she does, a ray of sunlight passes through the empty space that she leaves and hits the dragon's eye, igniting it, and – to me – it comes to life.

'It's alive!' I yell excitedly and point.

And, sure enough, the dragon looks straight at them. Pandemonium breaks out; girls are shrieking, one boy wets himself. Swiftly, Mr Simpson throws the cloth over the picture then tries to calm us all down.

'It's not alive. There are no dragons now in the Kingdom of Set. *There are no dragons*! They are all *dead*.'

He's saved by the bell ringing and the children escape the classroom. As he goes, Roland spits abuse at me, '*Dragonlover*' and the girl who sat next to me covers her ears and shakes her head as she leaves the room as if to shake out the words.

Mr Simpson makes me sit and wait for my mother. He turns his back and I lift a corner of the cloth that he's flung over the picture and touch the dragon. I trace around its coils and scales with my finger. I hear his voice behind me, horrified,
'What are you doing child?'
And I hear myself saying, 'How can something so beautiful be a monster?'
He steps back, whispering in shocked tones, 'You are a Dragonlover!' – just as my mother opens the door.

It's a long time since I've used that word. I love writing it – *Mother*.
My mother is –
was–

17

b e
aut
ifu
l.

Even in my memory, it's as if time slows down as she comes into the room and everything seems to revolve around her. She looks like butter wouldn't melt in her mouth but, as she opens the door, she takes in the scene at a glance: the look of horror on the teacher's face and me with my finger stopped mid-trace on the picture of the dragon. In one swift move she raises her staff. She always carried a long, straight staff made of ash – but this is the first time I've seen her use it to destroy anything. She brings it down and, with one blow, smashes the painting. As the glass shatters she seizes my hand and whirls me towards the door.

Mr Simpson is spluttering, 'You've just destroyed the rarest painting of...'

But my mother turns on him, 'How dare you show that to children!'

Simpson retaliates but his voice is shaking, 'Images which glorify our King in his moment of triumph over evil are...'

'Still dangerous and poisonous. I'm withdrawing my child immediately from such a corrupting establishment.'

Mr Simpson's face is as white as the chalk in his hand, 'And what of the child's reaction? He was crying for... for a...' he can barely whisper it, '...a *dragon*. I will have to report that to the School Board.'

'Three weeks in your class and you have already

poisoned the child's mind. I will demand your dismissal!'

'They can't dismiss me for using an official teaching aid.'

'But they will for corrupting a child's mind.'

Mother storms out, gripping my hand so tight I want to cry but something stops me. As we walk through the playground all heads turn. The whispers spread, fast and slippery, round and round, hissing like the snakes surrounding the school fence: 'Dragonlover, Traitor, *Sinsterine*.'

As we walk through the middle of them they start throwing the snakes. The first snake lands at my feet. I am terrified. So terrified I can't utter a sound. Mother grips my hand tighter.

'Hold your head up, Azra. That's *Rhamphotyphlops braminus*, the flower-pot snake, lives on termites and ants. Keep walking.'

There's a snake barrier around the playground so the playground is kept snake-free but there are always snakes in the trench the other side of the fence and they've harvested them. I know my mother works with non-poisonous *Asklepion* snakes, treating people with them, and her staff marks her out as a healer, but I am still terrified of them.

We walk on and the next snake lands on my shoulder. My mother loops it up with the hooked end of her staff and displays it in front of me as she recites, '*Leptotyphlops macrorhynchus*, thread snake, harmless, prefers to live underground.'

I feel the cold sweat on my face and I can't bring myself to open my eyes. My body starts to shiver but her voice soothes me.

'Open your eyes, Azra, just look.' And she makes me watch as she places it gently at the foot of a palm tree. 'See how beautiful it is.'

And she's right. It is really, really beautiful; its skin an almost translucent pink that changes, as it moves, to deep purple. I want to touch it – and this was where my fear of snakes begins to lose its grip on me – I do touch it.

'Most of the snakes around here are harmless; it's the humans that are the real danger. Look, it's searching for somewhere to hide, somewhere safe.' She glances across the yard at the parents collecting their children, their looks more venomous than the snakes they've thrown at us.

'Just keep calm, child. Fear is a greater enemy than anything they can throw at you.'

I place the snake under the tree and it disappears.

We continue our walk through the yard, my heart pounding in my chest as I keep walking at my mother's side and, with each step, I feel my fear changing, turning, inching its way into fascination.

'Did you know that a group of snakes is a nest or a bed?' She keeps up this conversational tone and now I know that it was to keep my mind occupied.

I am aware of every step I take, where every child and adult and snake is in that playground – most people are clustered by the gate. I am so focussed that, even now, I can see every one of those children really clearly as if I am there right now. I see the parents' lips moving as they pull their kids out of the way as if we are passing something on to them through the very air.

'A group of rattlesnakes is called a *rumba*,' I hear my mother say.

Now I have my eyes open as they throw the snakes, watching as she assesses them: whether they're poisonous or not, their age, their size. I start to recognise them.

Then I realise that all the kids throwing them are just as afraid of the snakes as I am; they hold them at arm's or stick's length, flicking them towards us. But now, what I see is very frightened kids and the snakes I see as, well, more like coloured ribbons and Mother is right: most of them – well, the snakes anyway – are harmless. With the dangerous ones, my mother turns her staff upside down, scooping them up with the hook, then grips the snake behind its head and hurls it over the fence.

Now, whenever I feel afraid, this is the memory I hold on to: clutching my mother's hand as we walk through the hail of snakes thrown at us from all sides. I hear her talking me through it, sizing up the danger and dealing with it. That is what she taught me that day- that there's nothing you can't get through in life if you take that approach; just face it, one step at a time.

We get into our horse-drawn station wagon.
'I knew I should have home schooled you. I'm sorry love.' She stops and looks at me

intensely. 'I thought we could do this. I thought that, as I'd hidden you this long, we were safe.'

It didn't make sense to me then. I had no idea what she was talking about until later, when things got much, much worse.

Our station wagon was like all the vehicles around here. They used to run on liquid but now they had been adapted. The place where we store things used to be for the machine called an engine, which used to turn the wheels, but I cannot understand how a liquid can be better than a horse. When the King banished fire, gradually all the machinery stopped working and we went back to using animals so now the horses pull the old cars that used to run on what they called petrol or diesel and the school bus has a team of six horses to pull it. That's why we say, 'There's no power to beat horsepower.'

Our horse's name is Rufus – such a dumb name for a horse but I loved that horse so I always think of a Rufus as reliable, dependable.

'What exactly did you do, child?' Mother asks.

'I said that I thought dragons are beautiful...'

She sighs a deep sigh, as if there is no hope left in the world. 'The truth is always difficult for some people. So they were teaching you about The Dragon Wars?'

'Yes.'

'Then I'll give you another view of them, my child. I'll give you the truth.'

Up the Chimney

As we drive through the school run rush my mother talks. She tells me more in that half hour than I think she has ever done in my whole life until then; and it is too much. It just sweeps over me and I don't understand half of what she says. She realises, looks down at me and her scarf falls away from her face so I can see her smile. I love the way she smiles; it feels like it is something she only shares with me for, outside, she always wears her scarf to conceal her scarred mouth

'It's all right, little one. Someday this will fall into place. You'll remember it when you need it.'

But eight years on it still hasn't come back so I think it's probably gone forever.

As we pull up, she jumps out. There are signs daubed in red on the door. She frowns as she pushes me inside and glances round as she ties Rufus to the hitching hook. I turn and see her touching the red, smelling it. She looks up at me, worried, and says, 'Blood.' The word seems to galvanise her into action. She runs around, grabbing stuff and comes to me with it and kneels before me. 'They are coming! We have no time. There is nowhere left for me to run to so listen, Azra. You know that I love you more than anything on this planet?'

I just stand there. I feel afraid. It petrifies me and I feel that if I keep as still and as quiet as I can it will all be better. I nod.

'So you must do as I tell you because no matter what you hear or see you must keep quiet. You understand?'

She's saying this to me and, at the same time, she's stuffing a cloth in my mouth, gagging me and tying my hands behind my back. And I let her do it! I just couldn't do anything else. This is my mother, my beautiful, lovely mother – okay, sometimes we yelled and argued but that was about things like not tidying my room or not washing my hands – this feels *totally different.*

–

And it is.

She hasn't finished when the banging starts on the door. Immediately, she picks me up and lifts me onto a ledge inside the ancient, disused chimney. She ties my feet and shoves a cushion under them.

'No matter what happens, no matter what they do to me, you must be brave and keep quiet. They are here to kill me, you understand?'

I feel myself choke on the gag as I try to cry out. I want to shout out, 'No, there's some mistake! They can't kill you! They don't know how great and wonderful and kind you are!'

'You must keep quiet or they will kill you too, my darling, and you have to live for all our sakes.' And what she said next I will always remember, for it terrifies me more than the walk through the snakes. *'For you have to bring the dragons back.'*

Instantly I am full of questions, 'What do you mean? Why me? How?' But they are to remain unanswered for I hear an axe, the unmistakeable sound of the wooden door splintering and heavy-booted men charging in. I am so terrified I pee myself. I am biting on the gag, crying and peeing.

I thought she had put the cushion there so that I would be comfortable – but that wasn't the reason. She knows that if there were the slightest sound they would find me. As I hear them, my body starts shaking and trembling, my feet pounding the cushion, and I am in serious danger of falling off the ledge. Dust and cobwebs spatter down around me – and that stops both them, and me.

'What's that?' demands the Shrill Voice. He sounds like he is shrieking the whole time.

My mother says nothing; there is just the sound of the slap as his leather glove hits her face.

He comes and thrusts his sword up the chimney. I hold my breath as he slashes it round but he hits a crow's nest that clatters down on top of him, the crow screeching and cawing, feathers, nest and dust landing on his upturned face, blinding him – and saving me. He backs off, cursing.

The shaking has stopped. It is as if the sense of danger has moved deep inside me as now I know how serious it is – and I have to be completely still.

I see a sliver of light on my shirt and follow it to a gap where the old mortar has long since fallen out from between the stones. I put my eye to it and can see two of them, soldiers, in the King's livery. They start circling round and then my mother moves into view. She's defenceless against them. I see the flash as the sword cuts through the air and she leaps aside, seizing her staff. The fighting is a blur of movement – my mother's white shift – their black leather and grey armour.

'We know you're a Dragon Keeper so you can stop pretending. This is the sword I stuck through your husband three years ago and I've been following your trail ever since. He squealed like a pig and told us everything. E-ver-y-thing.'

'Where is he? The child?' the Shrieker demands.

This was when I knew they knew nothing - and Mother did too. Father had not betrayed us.

The sound of feet, another soldier, three of them now, voices. 'Search upstairs.' Heavy, booted feet pound up to my room. They return.

'Where's the child? Where is he? We'll find him. You know that. We'll give you a quick death if you give us the child.'

Her face is towards me and I see her smile – almost –

so fleeting I wonder if I imagined it. She is happy that they don't know who I am. They are searching for a boy. That means that my father has kept me safe and now she will do the same. She knows that, for me, there's a chance. They even gave me a name that's more common for boys so even my name will help hide me.

I can't see. My eyes are full of tears and dust. I feel a guilty sense of relief – they know less than nothing.

But I don't have time to be relieved because they are killing my mother. And they are drawing it out, making her suffer. I hear the swish of the sword on cloth. I open my eyes and peer out – then close them fast. It makes no difference. Even with my eyes closed I can picture every sound. I hear them slash my mother's clothes, the soft fabric sliced, the sound of their swords thrust into her body, and I open my eyes to see her blood, bright red on the white linen. I have to be brave so I keep them open and watch. It's as if I am letting her know that I am still here, connecting with her. She makes no sound, only the involuntary gasp of pain as the sword enters. I see her eyes open and it's as if she has already left her body.

She knew they had come to kill us both and she's sacrificing herself for me. Her silence is to spare me.

I can hardly breathe. The gag is wet and thick in my mouth and my nose feels too small to keep me alive. Panic rises up in me, choking me. Like a monster sitting on my chest, it threatens me. 'Not now. Not now,' I think, desperately, look for a way to control this feeling.

Then I feel her. It's as if she is with me in the chimney, watching. I feel the closeness of her. Now the crow's nest has gone, a shaft of light streams in through the chimney and I remember the walk through the snakes. I am in no danger. My mother is keeping me safe. When the helplessness, knowing that I can't do anything for her, threatens me and the panic monster gains strength, I look up at the shaft of light. It's as if we are together in that shaft of sunlight and all the noise the men make, all their pig-like grunts, the fury, the thudding, slashing fury of them, becomes just background noise.

The Shrieker has stopped. I look into the room. The floor is a bloodied mess but my mother is no longer there, only her

empty body. I watch the light
and I feel her all around me.

On the Roof

They board up the house, all
the windows and doors, the
hammering pounding through
my head as I lapse into
unconsciousness.
I'm not sure how long I
was there, hidden in the
chimney. Granpa reckons it was
two days.

I remember no more until, late
at night, Granpa finds me and
hauls me, in a semi-conscious
ball, from my hiding place. The
room is empty; the only sign of
my mother her broken staff –
and the blood.

It takes weeks of Gramma's
herbal massages before my
body unfolds and begins to
return to normal. I don't want
to uncurl; I want to stay curled
up, foetus-like, forever.

That night we move, taking only what we stand up in, to the Rookeries. I keep looking for birds but Granpa says that it is called the Rookeries because it is so packed with people it's as noisy a rookery. I lie in the shade of my new bed on the roof of my grandparents' house in the heat of the afternoon, listening to the sounds of the Rookery – the voices, the music, people calling to each other – and to me they sound just like birds cawing. I like just listening to the sounds, not having to answer or be a part of it. Granpa says the people in the Rookeries are the salt of the earth but Gramma snorts whenever he says this, 'I can think of another name for them.' She never does say that name but Granpa is clear on this. 'These people are like you and me, Gramma Jonas. All of us here are the same. We have all had something terrible happen and are in hiding but we are all, at heart, decent citizens. One day this will be recognized and the Rookeries will be a place that people will favour again, as it was when it was built.'

Living in the Rookeries, I'm not unusual. Seeing my mother killed wouldn't make me stand out; most of the kids here have had a member of their family killed. Here I can fit in; it's a part of the city where no-one asks questions. Everyone here is running away from something so no-one talks about the past. But Granpa and Gramma still keep me hidden, even from the neighbours.

When I told them that the soldiers said they were looking for a boy they were so relieved. I am now allowed to dress like a girl and, after great debate, my Gramma stopped dyeing my hair. I was shocked when it grew out and I realized how red it is.

They have chosen the house carefully. It's separated from the others by an alley and at the back is a tiny garden where sometimes I'm allowed to walk. Mainly I live on the roof, hidden behind the great sandstone parapet, so all I can see is the sky. This is my window on the world and it is my friend. I love it from the first rays of the morning sun reaching out to kiss me and through the different moods of the day. Mostly it is brilliant blue and sunshine but then there will be a storm that will tear the sky apart with lightning and thunder followed, if I'm lucky, with a rainbow – until at night when the sky tucks me in under its dark, velvet, star-spangled blanket.

Granpa made my bed especially for me, with a rolling shelter for the few times in the year that the rain falls. I feel safe in this bed; it's like a big wooden nest for me.

My Gramma sewed my quilt and told me the story behind every piece – my mother's wedding dress, my father's cape, my christening gown – so in the cold desert nights I can close my eyes and feel that I'm wrapped up in the arms of my family.

At first, Granpa used to read me the stories that my mother read but Gramma didn't like the book, stories of the time before the Dragon Wars. One night she saw it and she was furious, 'Are you mad, old man? This stuff will get her killed.' She seized the book and tried to tear it apart but the pages started flapping and the book flew out of her old

43

woman's hands and up the chimney.

At any rate, that is how I remember it but maybe that is a dream. I started to store my memories as dreams because I had more control over them. I can change things in dreams that I can't in my everyday life – at least that is what I believed back then. Sometimes Gramma would sing to me, the songs my mother used to sing. She didn't do it often because it made her too sad to remember what she had lost, she told me.

The dragon stories were the one thing that helped me to sleep through the night. After Gramma took the book away I stopped sleeping through the night; I wet the bed again and the nightmares came back.

So Granpa gave me a journal to write in and told me to write the stories for myself, so I do. Each night I sit and

write in the magical world of
my journal then watch the
sunset and dream of a land
where the prince is kind-
hearted and the dragons come
back.

Death

Every morning, when the sun rises, it takes me some moments to realise that the world is the one that I left when I fell asleep yesterday. I help Gramma around the house and, since Granpa has now stopped going out to work, he shows me strange little tricks: taking in mouthfuls of water and blowing it out in streams, spinning and balancing sticks, tying ropes around me weighted with bean bags or containers of water. I play these games to humour him but he gets so angry with me sometimes. If I dribble any water down my chin or on my clothes he goes crazy, yelling in Scots, *'Ya careless bairn!'* Gramma reminds him he's never even seen Scotland so why talk in an ancient tongue to an innocent child? But, really, she wants him to stop doing these things with me so more and more he does them with me when she is napping or out on her occasional shopping trips.

That's when I think he's mad, that losing his daughter and having to hide his grandchild has touched him. I yearn for freedom but the thought of what lies out there keeps me safe in the nest of my hand-sewn quilt. I settle into this life, telling myself that they are my grandparents and I love them. That this is enough.

Each night as I finish writing my journal, *El Flacco,* the cat, comes at sunset and prowls my roof room as if he is guarding me throughout the night. I wake up to him licking my face, then he disappears for the rest of the day. I call him *my* cat but it is more a case of him looking after me; he is too independent to be owned. I feed him but I'm under no illusion that he wouldn't find food elsewhere if I stopped. I found him stuck in a drain culvert and Granpa reckons someone tried to drown him. At first, Gramma wouldn't let me keep him as a pet until she saw him fend off the fox that roamed our neighbourhood. She realised then that I was safer with *El Flacco* – the skinny one – than sleeping on the roof alone at night. He comes as the stars come out and sits on the parapet, keeping all the other cats and any scavenging birds away. Then, in the morning at sunrise, he comes and wakes me as if to say, 'My job's done, time to look after yourself'.

So it is, and has been, day in day out for the past eight years of my life – until one morning.

The day starts dull, the mist hanging over the desert for

longer than usual as if it is reluctant to leave. It is quiet and that silence has a strangeness in it. It comes to me that there is no sound from the kitchen.

Then I hear a sound, a strange sobbing. It comes from Gramma and Granpa's bedroom. I venture down from the roof to find that the door is ajar. The sobbing continues. When I open the door I see Granpa sitting by the side of the bed, the choking sobs are coming from him. His chest is struggling, reluctant to let the strange sounds out – and Gramma is staring at the ceiling, ash-white. He turns and takes control of himself, patting my hand.

'Ah child, she has gone. Gone. Perhaps she might be happier now. Maybe she will dance again with the angels. Now she's with your mother, God rest her.'

He looks at me as if seeing me for the first time. 'Now we need to do something about you, my not-so-little one. It is more fitting for you, a woman, to do this job than me. You are almost her nearest female relative.'

I look at him. 'Almost?' I query, 'Who else is there?'

'You will find out soon enough. I think the time has come.'

He hands me the bowl and cloth and I know what I must do. Gently, I squeeze out the cloth and start to wash the woman who for so many years had washed me.

The Dragon Keeper's Handbook

The funeral is a simple affair, just Granpa, me and the priest. Gramma is wrapped in a simple white shroud after I'd bathed her and the rites are in her native Arabic, which seems fitting. It is as it had been in life: we three cut off from the rest of society, trying to keep safe. Now, watching Gramma being lowered in her shroud into the dry earth, it feels that she at least will be safe in this secluded corner of the cemetery.

Granpa looks around the deserted graveyard, 'Ah child, there was a time when they would throng the streets for a glimpse of your Gramma.'

'Really?'

'She was the finest dancer that ever graced the

stage. She was so light she looked like a feather turning in the wind.'
'She never said anything.' I puzzle at this, then realize how Gramma never talked about the past. This was how she was able to live, not thinking of what had been and, even then, I could see it was painful for her sometimes when she looked at me.
'A dancer? On stage?'
'On stage, at court. That was where we met.'
'You were at court?'
What else did I not know about their lives?

There are other unmarked graves here and I hope, for the first time, that my mother might be one of them. I ask Granpa. He nods.
'Yes, I brought her here.'
He takes me to a spot not far from Gramma's freshly dug

grave. There is a slight mound under the cedar tree and, once I know what to look for, I can tell that it is a grave. I weep. My tears fall and I feel my Granpa restlessly looking around but I need this time; I have waited years for this moment.

The only thing to mark her grave is a stone, half-covered with a velvety green, the colour of my grandmother's old cloak. I touch it; it is so soft.

'What is this Granpa?'

'Moss or lichen,' he tells me, looking around all the time.

I roll the first word around in my mouth, '*Moss*' but '*Lichen*' I stutter and half choke on so I practise it. I kneel down and stroke it and it comes away slightly. I recoil in fright for the moss peels back to reveal the sign that I saw drawn in blood all those years ago, on our door.

'What is this sign?'

'A flame,' is all he says.

The word means nothing to me then. I have no idea what a flame is; to me it is just a shape etched into the stone. I run my finger around it and, as soon as I touch the stone itself, it begins to change shape. My heart stops and I can barely breathe as I feel the stone soften beneath my fingertips. It feels like leather. Shocked, I fall back.

I watch as the stone shape-shifts and bright brass glints in the sunlight. I look at Granpa in astonishment.

'It's turned into a book!'

Part of me wants him to tell me I am imagining it but he looks at it and sighs, 'It always was a book. It changes shape to hide itself. You had better pick it up, child. It is time.'

I pick it up and almost drop it in surprise at the weight.

'Careful, child,' Granpa Jonas admonishes me.

I open the leather and brass covers to reveal gold-edged pages that ripple and shimmer as if the words are eager to be read. The title page reads **The Dragon Keeper's Handbook** and beneath it a picture of a flame but this one is a glorious, shimmering red and gold.

'What is it? Was this my mother's?' I ask, excitement and curiosity overtaking my sadness.

'Yes, it was your mother's. It is what it says, child. And you must be ready because it will not show its true self to anyone but a true Dragon Keeper, one who is ready. It is a shape-shifter and has been disguising itself as a stone by your mother's side all these years.

'There are no Dragon Keepers. Gramma told me,' but I say this as if by rote, something I have learned. Even as I say it I know it isn't true because as soon as he tells me, no, even before that, the moment that I touched the stone I had felt it, the connection.

'That was what your Gramma told you in the hope that it would keep you safe. She thought that if you never thought of yourself as a Dragon Keeper then you could live a normal life.'

'Normal? From the day that I was born, my life has not been normal. Even my own mother disguised me as a boy – and that isn't normal. And it hasn't made me, or Gramma, or even you any less afraid, Granpa.'

He can't even look at me; he knows I speak the truth.

'I'm not a child, Granpa! I'm a woman.'

At this, he turns to look at me. 'And I can do no more for you.' He hesitates, reluctant, and then he says, 'Now we must go to the woods.'

He says it with resignation and gloom, but now I have *The Dragon Keeper's Handbook* in my hand and I feel that I have touched base, come home. A sensation that I'd almost forgotten comes over me; it feels as if my heart is singing – and, for a moment, it's as if my mother is by my side.

Corruption in the Palace

Granpa drives as I sit with *The Dragon Keeper's Handbook* in my lap. I had tried to leaf through it but some of the pages are bound together, though it feels more as if it won't let me.

The cover is mainly a kind of leather I have never seen before but part of it is still moss and lichen, soft as velvet to touch, growing – but why is it like this? As I think this, a page suddenly turns by itself and I read:

'My binding is made from the skin of the rarest of Dragons, the Octopus Dragon, so it is chromatophoric, enabling it to change to fit my surroundings.'

The book shuts itself, jumps out of my hands and spins around

in mid-air, showing off its
cover to me. I shout excitedly,
'Granpa, Granpa look!'
He clicks at the horse to
go faster so, by the time he
glances down at the book, it
has slumped heavily onto my
lap, grey and stone-like as I'd
found it. If a book can look
exhausted, this one did. Slowly
it opens itself and Granpa
watches in wonder.

'*The Handbook* is one of
the greatest mysteries and you,
child, are privileged that it is
letting you read it,' he says with
such feeling that I don't fully
understand until much later but
I hear the yearning in his voice
so I start to read from *The
Handbook* out loud:

*'Alas, so many years in the form
of a stone at your dear mother's
graveside has affected my*

chromatophores. I am having trouble adapting to new surroundings or, maybe, it is the fact that dragon magic is no more in this land. Hmmmmm.'

The '*Hmmm'* makes the whole book vibrate in my hands. This book - if that is really all it is - is alive! My mind is buzzing. How can it write this? I'm breathless with excitement. It writes as if it is talking to me, answering my questions!

'Of course I am! I am tuned in to your mind and your needs. I know what you need to know and what you are ready to know.'

I watch it carefully, not daring to move as it sits half-transformed: part moss and lichen-covered stone, part dragon-skin book. Questions race through my mind, 'What is an octopus dragon? Where are we going? Why is it letting me read it?' The print and pictures race across the page as fast as my thoughts, as if selecting the most important one. For an instant I see a beautiful dragon swimming in the depths of the ocean then, in an instant, it is transformed into a rock. Another page turns and the print settles:

'Only a Dragon Keeper can open me. Only a Dragon Keeper can read me. Only a Dragon Keeper's thoughts can imprint on me.'

For a moment I'm stopped in my tracks, almost afraid to think, but I cannot fathom anything for myself, so I read on...

The Dragon Keeper's Handbook

A History of Set

The official history of the Kingdom of Set states:

'The glorious Kingdom of Set once was the smallest kingdom on earth.

Since our great ruler, King Qahir –first called 'The Warrior King' – conquered the lands of the Dryseas, it has become apparent that this magnificent ruler, chosen and elected by the people of Set, reigns in the full glory of divine selection.

The terrible years of the Desert Storms and the Dragon Wars confirmed that King Qahir and the Settlers are the Chosen Ones, the only kingdom to survive on this planet Earth, now fondly renamed Qahir Terra by his grateful people in honour of King Qahir, Tyrranus Mundi – Ruler of the World and our Saviour.

King Qahir, by royal decree, has confirmed that Set is the chosen land and the Settlers – the native inhabitants of Set – the chosen people, are the only humans to survive the Desert Storms. At first it was thought these disasters were a sign of divine displeasure, invoked by the wrath of the gods at the Dragon Wars. Rumour had it that the gods were cutting the Kingdom of Set off from the rest of the world. So an expedition was appointed by the King to find any survivors beyond the Kingdom.

The exploration party comprised members representing every political interest, both the dissenters and supporters of the King. Before the Dragon Wars, when mankind and Dragon were allies, the Dragon Keepers flew, riding the Dragons. They were able to maintain contact with the rest of the world in this way – which, as only the Dragon Keepers were able to ride on the Dragons, meant the Dragon Keepers the most powerful class in Set. They conveyed messages between nations. They were called in whenever war threatened and, until the Dragon Wars, they were trusted and respected.

After the Dragon Wars, the only means of flight was with what some called Dragonflyers – officially they were called cyclopters. They flew using wings hewn from slain Dragons, painted in an attempt to hide their origins but everyone knew they were Dragon wings. These were attached to the cyclopter – a complicated system of pulleys and wheels that were operated by the pilot. The pilots were the fittest athletes in the Kingdom and they needed all their strength to power these complicated machines. This expedition force was sent to the four corners of the earth to find any signs of human life. Soothsayers predicted disaster for this mission on account of using Dragon wings. Alas, they proved right at great cost to the explorers; only one returned alive and able to speak. A second returned an imbecile, so traumatised was she by the horrors she had seen.

What was certain, and the only information allowed to be reported, was that the rest of the world had been destroyed by a series of tsunamis, volcanic eruptions and other natural disasters. No humans survived the catastrophe beyond the now land-locked Kingdom of Set.

Wild animals roamed the earth, monsters from deep within the ocean had swept onto land by the tsunamis and had quickly adapted to their new environment. Rumour had it that it was these creatures who had devoured the rest of the expedition. The tales were recorded for the Palace archive but so terrible were the stories that it was said that the scribe who recorded them was driven mad by the atrocities, as would anyone who read them, so the book was sealed and buried in the caves below the Castle.

One thing was now clear – The Desert Storms had created a barrier that had protected the Kingdom and now what had been viewed as a disaster was seen as having saved the Kingdom of Set.

Geographically, Set once encompassed every climate and landscape found throughout the world. The Dryseas were the only route to the sea and the source of fish and salt for the Settlers. These vast desert lands were so desolate that the Settlers referred to them as 'The End of the World. The name proved all too prophetic as the series of volcanic eruptions and subsequent sandstorms destroyed the only land route through the Dryseas so they did become the end of the world and the Settlers the only humans to survive this catastrophe.

Settlers told tales of the old days when Set was a bubbling hive of activity, an oasis that sat like a jewel in the desert, with traders from all around the world journeying to this thriving place. But, within a short time, these tales began to sound, even to the tellers, the stuff of myth and legend and too devastating to contemplate the reality of what lay beyond what they now saw as the comfort and safety of Set. There were some who said they believed that there is still life beyond the Dryseas but no-one has spoken out loud of this... and lived.

King Qahir reigns supreme: Tyrranus Mundi – Supreme Ruler of the World – but, in his attempt to appear modest, King Qahir insists on the more familiar title of King Qahir to show his closeness to his people. So, often, on state

69

occasions when the herald proclaims his titles, the King will smile and insist that he be addressed by the simpler and more familiar title of King Qahir.

The vast City of Set is now a warren of abandoned mud-brick houses and the division between the Palace and the City is so great that the Palace courtiers never dare set foot in the City for fear of the wrath of the City-dwellers. The only communication between City and Palace is the soldiers who patrol the City to enforce the dictates of King Qahir. Though none dare tell the reality of this state of affairs to the King.'

'Why do the courtiers fear the city dwellers, Granpa?'

His reply makes me realise how hard it has been for him.

'Since the King banned fire he has made life in the city unbearable. We cannot work the way we used to. We cannot cook. We have to go to bed when it gets dark.' The bitterness sounds in his words. 'The city folk blame him and anyone connected with the palace.'

And here is Granpa caught between the two – banned from the palace and not accepted by the city folk.

'The Palace itself is an exotic timber building, hewn from the great Forest of Content. The Forest was established by King Qahir's great, great grandfather, Khalil Qualtrough, a visionary ruler

who devised a watering system that utilised the water from the volcanic springs beneath the Palace and the wastewater from the City. It was a beautiful forest and named The Forest of Content as it provided enough food to supply the City and the Palace. It teemed with deer and game and had many ponds, saving the arduous and hazardous journey across the Dryseas for fish. So the Kingdom was integrated to be a self-sufficient biosphere, providing all the Settlers needed for their daily food.

But building work by Khalil Quatrough has depleted the Forest and the creation of a moat around the Palace by Chancellor Vlast has drained the ponds.

Water is now a major problem for the City. Now the desperate need for water means that the wastewater is being filtered for reuse in the City and the Forest of Content is dying from lack of water.'

'But this isn't anything special! This is boring. It's just history. You used to tell me this story when I was a child!'

'Yes, Azra, but every story is different each time it is told and each time you hear it you will hear something different and understand more. *The Handbook* must need you to understand it. Read on. It is telling you something.'

I turn the page to reveal a 3D map showing the vast, desolate extent of the Dryseas. It takes up two thirds of the map and there, in the bottom third, lies the Kingdom of Set. It shows the palace built atop the mountain and how the Forest of Content separates the palace from the city. It makes me feel tiny, this insignificant little place that is my home is so small on the map. I try to show Granpa. He looks but he just shakes his head, he cannot see anything within *The Handbook's* pages.

Then I look again. Suddenly I see it all. What was once just words is now clearly laid out for me. On the map, Khalil Quatrough's purpose is clear: the forest is meant to *connect* the city and the palace; the water piped from the volcanic springs beneath the palace was intended to supply the city while the sewage from the city would water and feed the forest that would provide food for everyone. It seems so obvious I don't understand why anyone would ever dream of changing it. Why did they take the water for a palace moat? I must have spoken out loud for Granpa looks down at me sharply.

'I told you there was something in there for you to see, child. There is corruption afoot in the palace and it has gone on too long. It was right under my nose when I was there but I didn't see it. You have.' He chucks me under the chin, something he hasn't done since I was small, and I know I've done something smart when he does that.

The Dragon Keeper's Handbook
The Dryseas

'The Dryseas were ruled by the Al Watan Al `atshaan, which roughly translates as 'The Nation of Thirst'. This nation consisted of small nomadic tribes or family groups of ten to twenty people. These once fierce warring tribes had united under the leadership of the Sheikh Abu – who the Al Watan Al `atshaan called 'Father'.*

After the Great Divide, these lands became uninhabitable, even for this hardy people, so they came and dwelt on the borders of Set. These fierce tribes were renowned for their horses, beautiful creatures that they

76

bred and trained. Their skills in horsemanship were legendary and King Qahir craved this for his stables. Sheikh Abu fiercely resisted any approach by King Qahir to acquire any of his trainers or breeding animals so it was only on the untimely death of Sheikh Abu and King Qahir's subsequent marriage to his widow, Sheikha Esther, that the Al Watan Al `atshaan and their horses were *assimilated into the Kingdom of Set. This was called King Qahir's most peaceable conquest.'*

Granpa snorts – and I stop and stare at him in surprise.
'What is it?'
'It wouldn't read like that in my hands.' He shakes his head. 'They've rewritten history and left the real people

out. "Untimely death", when the whole of Set knew that the King had him done away with.'

'He murdered her husband and she married him?'

'The ways of politics are not what ordinary folks would care for but who is to know how her first husband treated her? For the Sheikh could be a brutal man too.'

He refused to be pressed any further, so I read on:

'The Al Watan Al `atshaan *and their Sheikha-turned-Queen adapted, on the whole, with surprising readiness to court life.'*

'Hah! As if they had any choice in the matter,'Granpa complains. 'Who is writing this stuff, anyway?'

'I don't know – it doesn't say.'

78

'Are you sure?'

I search the cover but there is no name inscribed. Then, as I turn to the *Contents* page, my heart skips a beat. There is a list of all the chapters and beside each one is the name of the Dragon Keeper who wrote it. At the bottom, second chapter to last under the heading *The Dragon Wars,* is a name that makes me gulp. The last chapter is *Return of the Dragons* and I feel a bubble rising up inside me. The sob gushes from my mouth and explodes out.

Granpa stops and pulls over. 'There, there child,' he comforts me. I must have shocked him because he's never been so gentle with me. 'What is it? What did you read?'

I'm still choking, the grief is filling my mouth and throat, and I cannot speak for sobbing. He holds my hand and crushes my teary face with his rough old hands to his shoulder; the coarse rough jacket is so like him, even his attempt to be gentle is rough, it makes me smile through my tears. I wipe my face.

'The last two chapters – they're Mother's. She wrote them.'

A deep understanding and sadness passes between us and we sit, holding hands in silence; the only sound the throaty call of the desert lark. Then its mate replies, a distant far-off sound, but it gives me hope. A lingering tear falls onto the page and magnifies the A in my mother's name – Agnes Jonas. The birds call again to each other – a call, a reply and, for a moment, I feel a warmth, a glow that I am not alone, that my mother is with me.

Granpa clicks his tongue and Rufus moves on. The sun

shines onto *The Handbook* and the page turns, it has another story for me and I let it flick – I have no choice!

'One moonlit night, the King and Queen were walking along the Palace battlements. As they watched, a shooting star blazed its trail across the clear, dark blue sky and the stars glistened, bright as diamonds. The Queen clutched the King's arm. 'I wish, I wish for a child!' She turned to the King and said, 'You must wish too and it will come true.'

So King Qahir looked into the longing in his Queen's eyes and then up at the star. 'I wish for a son as wise as his mother and as strong as me.''

I wish with them and I hope it will come true.

'So she loved him.'

'Why do you say that, child?'

I'm startled at his tone. He looks so angry; his pale face is vivid and the veins on his neck pulse a dark blue.

'Because she wants to have a baby with him. This is a great love story, Granpa!'

'Love! Ah child, it is not as simple as that. I had seen him look with love on another and to see him shift his affections was terrible to witness....'

I want to question him more, his anger has softened, but now he looks close to tears. He brushes his watery eyes and gives me a weak smile. 'I suppose you are right, child. I think she did grow to love him and he grew to love her. I could see it in the way he watched her.'

'You knew the King?' I can hear the surprise in my own voice – how little I know about my grandfather even though I have spent almost every day of the past eight years of my life with him.

'Aye lass, I was at court for many years.'

'What did you do at court, Granpa?'

But Granpa seems uncomfortable; he doesn't want to talk about it.

'That's a story for another day. This one is the story that needs to be told now.'

I get so mad. 'I'm an adult now, Granpa. Stop hiding things from me.'

'You're still only fifteen, child and this isn't about hiding things from you, this is the official story,'

He taps his finger on *The Handbook*. 'It's what you need to know for your own good and protection. If *The Handbook* thinks this is what you need then we need to stick with that. The family story is another matter.'

I can see that it's all I'm going to get out of him but by now I'm really into the story so I continue:

'...Nine months later, the Queen gave birth to the most beautiful baby boy. His skin was the colour of ripe peaches, his legs were fine and strong and he had a loud, hearty cry. The Queen smiled when she heard it for that cry had the strength of life in it. But the poor Queen knew that giving birth had opened up an old

84

*wound deep inside her and this
took all her strength from her.'*

'I don't want to go on
Granpa.'
'Why not, child?'
'Because it feels sad and
I've gone all cold inside.'
'It is sad, my precious.
But sometimes you just have to
go through the sad times.'

*'The Queen was so weak that
she could barely speak so the
King knelt by her bed so she
could whisper in his ear,
'Promise me, my beloved, you
must promise me that you will
celebrate the birth of our son
with the best birthing party
ever.'*
*'Of course I promise,
dearest,'he told her.*

Then he saw it in her eyes, the light fading. Desperately, he tried to hold on to her but she told him, 'Y o u must not mourn for me but take strength in our child for he is the product of our love and he will thrive on love.'

He knew that she was dying and he could only nod and weep for this marriage brought about by murder and betrayal had changed them both and had grown into true love. So he buried her quietly, alone. And, true to his word, he threw a great party for the new Prince that went on for five days and five nights.

They travelled from all five corners of the Kingdom of Set, arriving travel-worn and weary, bearing gifts for the newborn. Everyone dressed in

*his or her finest clothes –
laughing, drinking, toasting.*

*In the centre of the Great
Hall stood the crib, beautiful to
behold for his mother had made
it with her own hand. She had
sought out the most luxurious
palm fronds, the finest olive
branches and the supple young
stems of the sacred terebinth
oak from the Forest and woven
them into an intricate pattern.
Laced in amongst these
branches were precious stones
and crystals that looked like
flowers glowing and growing
amongst the branches so they
caught the light, creating
playful patterns that made the
baby Prince laugh and chuckle.*

*The baby gurgled and
laughed in his beautiful crib
while all around him was the
murmuring sound of strange*

tongues. *But they all had one thing in common; they all had something to give. One by one they leant over his crib and presented the child with a gift and made a speech. Each gift was more generous than the last and each speech more and more elaborate as the gift-givers competed with one another to bestow the best and greatest blessings on the child.*

As the ceremony drew to a close there was a disturbance at the gate.

Voices were raised and the noise reached the ear of the King.

'What dissension is this on our day of celebration?'

The guard hesitated, this strange creature looked like a bundle of rags yet talks with the voice of an educated woman.

'Sire, this...lady seeks admittance. She says she is invited but has no invitation.'

'Let her in, let her in.' The King was too busy watching the reaction of his fine guests to his magnanimity – the great King Qahir admitting a beggar to the celebration– to take much notice of the woman, otherwise he too might have hesitated.

A white-haired woman, bent almost double, twisted with a bitterness that was awful to see, came and leant over the crib. She looked at the child and a sigh escaped her lips. She turned and looked directly at the King.

'You do not remember me, sire?'

The courtiers muttered and speculated who she could be.

'I know you not, old woman,' the King replied but a trace of uncertainty crept across his face.

'Old! You call me old?' she cried out haughtily in her rage. 'There was a time when you did not think me old...then you gave me a gift.' She held out her crabbed fingers to show a ruby ring that glittered red and caught the light. As the light from the ring flickered and passed over the courtiers it was as if a fleeting memory stirred throughout the Court.

Lord Vruntled said, 'I seem to remember a rumour that the King was secretly engaged to another before he met his Queen. And this...' Lord

Vruntled put in his eyeglass for a clearer view, '...could this must be she?"

Granpa stops the horse and looks even sadder than when Gramma died. I stop reading and put my arm around his shoulders to try to comfort him but he says,
    'Ah child, may you never have the tears I have bottled up inside me. For longer than you've been on this earth I've held them, my pride and anger keeping them back. I wasn't there for my child when she needed me the most. This story that you are reading must be what you need to see right now or maybe it is what I need to hear but it is not the tale as I would tell it.' He strokes my cheek and sighs a sigh with decades of regret in it.

'You best read on before we meet your aunt. Then you can judge for yourself.'

'My AUNT? I have an aunt?'

'Yes, your mother's sister, but we haven't spoken since you were born,' he pauses, suddenly struck by the thought, 'I don't even know if she is still alive.'

It feels like he's slapped me across the face. I take a deep breath but he says,

'Go on.'

I glance down at the page. I'm finding out more in this book than I have done from him. The book reads differently now, it's less pompous, more real, it now reads like I'm *there*!

The Dragon Keeper's Handbook

'The whole Court waited with bated breath as the woman stooped over the crib, casting a shadow over the child. In a cold voice that sent a shudder down your spine she cried out for all to hear,

'I will give your child a gift, a prophecy: He will destroy both you...' She pointed at the King and a single ray of red light darted from her ring towards his heart, '...and the Kingdom of Set with fire before the sun sets on his sixteenth birthday.'

Before the startled Court could recover, she seized a burning brand from the wall and set fire to the carpet at the King's feet.

The cry went up to seize her but she disappeared in the blink of an eye, slipping past the fire in the great hearth and up the chimney.

Pandemonium broke out as the fire surged around the King's feet but it was he who recovered first. He flipped the rug over on itself, quenching the flames. The immediate danger was over but the entire Court was hysterical – until the King's command rang out,

'Silence! Put out every fire, every torch, every flame.'

At his command, the soldiers quenched the flames of all the burning torches that lined the Palace walls. Each and every fire in the Palace was extinguished and, with every shovel of sand and every torch snuffed out, the lights went out and the laughter died. The setting sun cast its dying rays through the Palace windows as the King declared, 'From this day forward, all fire is banished from this Palace.' He paused and decided it was not enough, 'Fire is banned throughout the Kingdom of Set!'

A horror spread around the whole Court as, slowly, it sinks in, what life will mean for them without fire. But the idea was only an inkling of the reality of life without fire.'

I turn to Granpa. 'Why did they think it would be so terrible to live without fire?'

'Ah Azra, you have never known how wonderful life is *with* fire, how food tastes, how we struggle to keep warm at night, we could not repair our machines or make new ones and, more important, what the King did not realise is that when he banned fire in the world, it also put out the fire of love in our hearts. We live in a cold, heartless land compared to when we had the fire of love in our hearts and fire in our hearths. Words cannot teach what that is like you have to experience it.'

I hate it when he talks like this, of things that I cannot ever experience. It is so unfair. All I have is this book. Grumpily, I jolt it on my knees and it cries out,

'Ow!'

'Sorry.'

A page turns and I settle down, careful not to jolt the book again.

'It's not my fault what happened.

Anyway, to continue, King Qahir then went on to pronounce that anyone found

with a flame of any kind would be exiled.

At this, Lord Vruntled turned and whispered to Lord Pacatore, 'The King has mellowed with age. At one time it would have been a beheading.'

However, the King makes the punishment clear, 'Exiled to the Dryseas.'

A ripple of fear ran through the Court and Lord Pacatore shuddered. 'Personally I think a beheading is preferable to an excruciating death in the Dryseas.'

Lord Vruntled nodded in agreement.'

'Lord Vruntled and Lord Pacatore! I wonder what they are up to these days?'

As Granpa speaks, the book comes to life, the pages flick rapidly and re-open at a pop-up of the palace. Granpa glances down, pulls on the reins and halts Rufus in astonishment. He looks at me in wonder.

'I can see. I can read. I can...' He sniffs delightedly. 'I can even smell, what is in *The Handbook*!' he exclaims.

From the pages emerge the sound of eating and sizzling, along with a glorious smell.

The old man sniffs, his nose picking up the delightful smells that he has missed for so long.

'What's that smell Granpa?'

'Ah, bacon!' He sniffs out more, eagerly following his nose. 'Sausage!' The smells overcome the awe he has at being able to read what is in

The Handbook. He delves into the pages of the book, tracing the smells through the corridors of the palace, deep, deep down into the underbelly of the underground caverns and kitchens. The book reveals itself to him and, with such great delight, he lifts up the tiny pop-up rooms to reveal a scene of gluttony and greed. 'A Breakfast Club! Ah there they are, those wily rascals.'

'When the King banned fire, the repercussions were felt far and wide. The lack of fire meant that nothing could be cooked. The basic things that all Settlers had taken for granted – a fire to keep them warm in the cold desert nights, light to cast away the darkness, heat to cook food and water – all that was

gone, banned. A traditional Settlers breakfast had been, from time immemorial: scrambled eggs, falafel, hummus, pitta bread and fried beans. Since the Scottish influence, the hearty breakfast of a hunter-farmer also introduced crisp fried pork slices, or bacon as Granpa called it, sausage and, for those with less hearty appetites, cooked oats or porridge, bread or toast.'

'We still have bread now, Granpa,' I told him.

'Rock-bread baked on stones warmed by the sun is very, very different to a yeasty bread, plump and fresh-baked in an oven, child.' He reaches into the book and picks up the tiny loaf from the baker's peel as the tiny baker takes the bread from the oven. The tiny loaf is red-hot and Granpa juggles it until it cools and, as he does, the bread seems to grow in size. He passes it to me, indicating that I should eat it.

I blow on it. It's so hot I fear it will burn my mouth. I tear a piece off and Granpa has cut a chunk of yellow butter from the book and spreads it on my bread. It melts immediately in the heat. I pop it in my mouth and boy oh boy! It's crumbly and hot and melting at the same time. It tastes *totally* different to rock bread. My eyes feel like they're popping out of my head. I have never, ever in my life eaten anything this hot!

'Different, huh?' says Granpa.

I just nod, eyes watering. It's not just the heat of the bread, it's so moreish! For the first time I have a glimpse of what we have lost. Until now I have known no different but they were used to this every day and, if Granpa is right, this is just a small part of what we have lost.

'So those wily rascals have a breakfast club going in the palace. I wonder how they get away with that, perhaps because they clamp down so hard on any underground eating clubs in the city?'

'There are eating clubs in the city?'

'There used to be lots but, because the rewards for informing on them were so great and the penalties for being found in one so harsh, they have almost all disappeared. So read on, child, let's find out what's afoot in the palace.'

'The ban on fire was enforced harshly and rigorously by King Qahir and, while he occasionally felt twinges of regret that he would never taste roast venison or drink hot coffee again, he knew it was for the greater good; to protect not only himself but the whole Kingdom. The people, he was certain in his own mind, supported him in this; the whole Court was behind him – or so he believed until one bright morning...

This morning the King wakes early, exceptionally early – and he wakes hungry so he calls for his manservant who is nowhere to be seen. He wanders through the deserted corridors, down the stairs, past the sleeping guards and into the Palace kitchens. There is no-one there, except the kitchen boy sleeping under the table.

'Boy!' the King yells and nudges him with his foot. T h e kitchen boy wakes with a start and something falls with a clatter from his fingers. The King picks it up, examines it and smells it, curious. It smells familiar. He knows this smell. He sniffs again and the answer forms into words, 'Chicken. Cooked chicken!'

Anger rises up within him, bubbling and boiling. He pokes the chicken-bone into the kitchen boy's face. 'Where did you get this?' he bellows.

The kitchen boy is dumb-founded. No-one more senior than the cook had ever spoken to him and this is the King! But he had been taught well, to speak only when he is spoken to *and to do as he is told – so he does both.*

'Er, in the cellar kitchen, sire.'

'Take me there at once!' bellows the King.

The kitchen boy leads the way along the winding corridors, down the stairs, along the dark, dank hall into the bowels of the Palace. As they stand outside the door, a wisp of steam curls out of the keyhole along a shaft of light, wafting faint but distinct smells to the King's nostrils– meat!

The smells assail his nose and more follow. His nostrils twitch – Is it? Yes it is! Even in his rage, the King's mouth waters at the smell of hot, buttered toast.

The King turns the kitchen boy around so that he

cannot see the undignified posture of His Royal Highness bending his royal knees and peering through the keyhole – And what a sight greets him!

Fiery torches blaze around the windowless walls. The table is groaning with a breakfast banquet of cooked meats: roast venison, camel, chicken and steaming bowls of hot potatoes. There's the sound of greedy guzzling.

Lord Pacatore, with a dishevelled kitchen maid on his lap, his plump little body quivering with excitement, seizes a chicken leg with one hand and tears it off while his other hand grabs and juggles a hot steaming potato. He munches as if his life depends on it.

There is barely a sound through the heavy oak door but when the kitchen boy, nudged by the King, opens the door and falls in, the raucous sound of guzzling, chomping, slobbering and gutsy laughter bursts out. For one second, the air is bombarded with noise – that fades as fast as the fleeing breakfasters at the sight of the King. The dishevelled motley crew of feasting courtiers and servants disappear: into barrels, down trapdoors, behind wine-racks. The boldest slithering behind the King and out the door. The King stands, taking it all in. He realises that if he banished all those present to the Dryseas he would lose the best – and last – cook in the Kingdom, half the Palace Guard as well as almost his entire Court. But he can not be seen to be weak.

Then the solution presents itself in the shape of the portly belly of Lord Pacatore protruding from behind a barrel, accompanied by Lord Vruntled's long, pointy-toed shoes sticking out beneath the wine rack that they have hidden behind.

'Vruntled! Pacatore!'

They emerge from their hiding place and Vruntled, as usual, takes charge.

'Sire, sire, I can't believe this. We stumbled upon this place this morning and were just collecting the evidence to present to your Majesty.'

So saying, he holds out the half-eaten haunch of venison in his hand as he bows so low and obsequiously that his hair sweeps the floor.

This infuriates the King even more, his face turns first red then purple with rage. *'Blithering idiot! Do you take me for a fool?'*

'No, no sire.'

'Oh but you do! Running a Breakfast Club under my roof! How dare you! Then having the audacity to try to pass it off as something you have just stumbled across. Well, enough is enough. You are banished...'

'But Sire...'

'...to the Dryseas.'

The little blood left in Vruntled's skinny face drains away and he drops to his bony knees. *'I beg you, Sire.'*

He looks so pathetic that the King has to stop himself

from leniency. He turns his gaze on Pacatore, whose rotund body is quivering like a jelly. 'And you too. You will be company for each other at your deaths as well as in your miserable, misspent lives. Guards!'

Silence greets this.

'Guards!' At this second, furious command the chains and the wine bottles rattle. It makes the rats scurry and shakes the walls so the cobwebs quiver and dust falls from the ceilings. There is a thunder of boots and clink of armour as the guards hurry to obey.

They look to the King, who turns to the two miserable, once-proud Lords, grovelling at his feet.

'The Dryseas,' is all he says. Then he turns to go and

smiles to himself as he says,
'Take them in the old Meat-
wagon.'
    'A nice touch,' he thinks
to himself and it puts him in a
good mood for the rest of the
day.'

The next page is blank.
Something is puzzling me,
    'Granpa, why is *The*
Handbook writing in the
present?'
    He looks at me and I see
realisation dawn on him.
'Thank goodness for your
young mind, child.' He gees
Rufus to move on. 'We need to
get to the forest, child.'
    'What's so urgent?'
    'This is happening now.'
    'How can you tell?'
    '*The Handbook* is
writing in the present...'
    I burst out, 'Is that why
we can eat the food?'

'I guess so. But, more important, the Prince's birthday banners were on the table.'

I glance at the picture. There are the banners lying in the kitchen – *Happy Sixteenth Birthday, Prince Samardashee* – and I know he is right, what was history in *The Handbook* is now the present.

'They're preparing for his birthday.'

'When is his birthday, Granpa?'

'The same day as yours, child.'

The time of the prophesy is at hand. I feel an excitement I cannot explain that overrides any fears that I have. I can feel the fear in Granpa, but it is not mine. Something tells me that I am about to meet with this mysterious prince who shares my birth date. My head tells me I should be afraid but my heart tells me these are exciting times. I feel my fears are in the past and I look towards the unknown future with real excitement.

The Forest of Discontent

I follow behind Granpa as he makes his way through the Forest. I had started to felt uneasy when he first told me to pack my bags and when I asked where we were going he would only say, 'You'll see.'

Whilst I was kneeling on my bed packing an old backpack that he had dug out from somewhere, Granpa dropped the bombshell. He told me he had taught me all he could; now it was time for me to go and finish training as a Dragon Keeper. I knew he had lost the plot, Gramma's death had been the last straw, so I told him gently that there are no dragons and there is no need for me to be a Dragon Keeper.

He didn't answer me, just picked up his axe and said, 'Get off the bed.'

Shocked, I obeyed without protest. I knew he wouldn't hurt me but, even so, my heart was pounding when he tossed the mattress aside and raised his axe.

'Stop!' I screamed so loud my ears rang, tears streaming down my face. I tore at his sleeve. He couldn't do this; this bed was my den, my safe place and my hidey-hole. Even if I went away I wanted to know that it was still here, waiting for me. But he couldn't stop. The axe was already swung and the momentum smashed it into the bed. The wood groaned and splintered.

'It's served its purpose,' he gasped.

He had to pause for breath so I seized my chance but the moment I tried to wrest the axe from him it was as if he dug deeper and found more strength.

'If you want me to go I'll just go but don't destroy my bed, Granpa.'

He looked at my tear-streaked face and took pity on me. 'Azra, it's not just your bed. I made this as a safe hiding place...'

His next stroke split the bed and he stood aside to reveal what looked like a stone, blue-grey with hints of green. I looked at him, puzzled.

'It's a dragon's egg. They need to be kept warm the whole time, 24/7, to keep them alive. I hid it here so your body heat would keep it warm at night and the heat of the sun would keep it warm in the daytime. It was the only way. Your mother asked me to.'

I looked at him, stunned. Suddenly everything fell into

place and fell apart at the same time. So the whole time this was about the dragons, not me. All those days when it was foggy and Granpa persuaded me to come up to my bed and draw the curtains around it; I thought that was for me but it was all for the dragon. I thought my bed was up here on the roof so the stars would comfort me. Gramma used to tell me my mother was one of those stars looking down on me, watching over me. But now? I felt like I was nothing, that I was totally unimportant; my whole life had been for one thing – and one thing only – keeping the dragon alive.

'But you built this bed after I came here. So where was it before?'

'Yes, it was a miracle they never found it. They ripped open the mattress in your crib but not the crib itself.

That's why I made your bed this way, so it would have to be destroyed to even see the egg.'

I felt the salt from my tears drying on my face as my sorrow turned to anger.

'Did Gramma know?'

He shook his head. 'I was afraid she would destroy it. She was so bitter at the death of your mother. But this is what your mother would have wanted.'

'Would she? She gave her life for *me*! I *know* that. I *saw* it. It wasn't just for a stupid egg.'

'Of course not, but you must understand she was a Dragon Keeper and this was the only way she had left to try to save her dragon. It should have been her job to teach you to be a Dragon Keeper.'

I could see his eyes fill with tears but even that didn't

stop the anger when he told me, 'I've taught you all I can.'

'What? What have you taught me? Stupid sword games with sticks? How to spit water?'

I was boiling up inside, the anger pouring out of me, that all these years he has hidden me, kept things from me. I thought he was keeping me safe but it's some stupid dragon's egg that he's been hiding all this time.

He looked so hurt as I yelled at him but I didn't care. I wanted him to feel what it was like to have your whole life taken from you, to be belittled and made to feel worthless. I thought I hadn't much before, but now... now I felt I had nothing. It made all the times we spent together feel worthless, as if all the joy has been taken out of them.

I watch, sullenly, as he gathers bottles and potions

from Gramma's store and packs them along with the egg.

It didn't make me feel good at all screaming all this stuff at him, but I couldn't say I was sorry because I wasn't – I wanted him to suffer too.

Then, as I yelled at him, my mother's last words come back to me, 'You have to live for all our sakes; you have to bring the dragons back.' And that's what shut me up.

So here we are, in the Forest of Discontent, and my feeling of discontent deepens as we walk through its dark, tangled stench and fear hits my stomach like a cold, wet ball.

He seems to know where he is going, though how, I don't know. How long it is since he has been here I can only guess but I am sure he hasn't been here since I have lived with him and Gramma. He has brought his axe and he needs it to hack a way through the tangle of undergrowth. At one point we find a signpost fallen on its side that reads 'Tinker's Cottage.'

'What's a tinker?' I ask.

'It's someone who mends all the broken pots and pans and metalwork – a difficult trade without fire.'

'And why do we need to find him?'

'We need him to find your aunt.'

'And this tinker will know where she lives?'

'Maybe, maybe not. Who knows if either he or she is still alive? The world is full of uncertainty and unanswered questions. Ah, child! Questions, questions – and I can't ever give you a decent answer without stirring up the past and some things that are best left unstirred. But you won't be in the dark much longer, more is the pity.'

I feel a chill in the pit of my stomach as he says this and I wonder if knowing really can be worse than not knowing?

We continue through the forest, winding through the undergrowth and over and around fallen trees. The smell changes as we move in deeper; the stench has gone and the scent of eucalyptus fills the air. Gradually, the undergrowth becomes less dense; it looks as if someone is taking care of this part of the wood. We come into a clearing – and there it is, the Tinker's Cottage.

I have never seen anything like it; it is made of wood, like a big box with a sloping lid for a roof and a porch. A stack of wood that looks as though it has been there longer than I have been alive stands to one side: a black mirror is clipped onto the roof, tilted up to the sky. Other piles of junk, metal and glass lie under the eaves, shaded from the sun.

A tall, broadshouldered man works under the shade of the porch at a lathe, making a bowl. The shelves beside him are stacked with finished bowls of all sizes, alongside spoons and ladles. Granpa watches him at work for a while before making himself known.

'Tinker,' he says as he approaches the man.

The man looks up at him, slowly, and gradually eases his foot off the lathe. 'No-one has called me that in years.'

'I suppose it's not appropriate these days? I never knew your given name, you were only ever *Tinker* at court.'

The man grunts, a mixture of agreement and dissatisfaction. 'I prefer my given name these days, it brings me less trouble – Rufus.'

I immediately warm to him and, in my eyes, he now has the solid reliability of my old horse. He holds out his hand.

'So, Jonas, what brings you here?'

Granpa holds out his axe.

'For me?' Rufus looks surprised and pleased, then doubt clouds his face. 'What do you want in exchange for such a valuable gift?'

Granpa shakes his head. 'Information – but this is yours whether you can help me or not. You can put it to better use than I; my time is almost out.'

Rufus looks at him quizzically then shakes his head as if he has second thoughts about probing deeper. His gaze falls on me.

'And who is this?'

'This is my grandchild, Azra.'

He looks at me closely. 'The red hair of the Mackenzies,' is all he says. Then he smiles. 'I'll accept this, Old Jonas,' he says, taking the axe. 'But as a keepsake; I'll look after it for you.' He says all this while looking at me. 'You look as though you could both do with a good meal.'

He was right, we hadn't really eaten properly since Gramma died and we were both skinny at the best of times.

Rufus picks up three bowls – one has the sheen of being well-used – and leads us round to the side of the clearing where the sun blazes down. The earth is parched and dry here and, in the middle, stands a big box with a glass lid. He opens it and I have to shade my eyes – it is silver inside and it reflects the sun, dazzling me. In it is a cooking pot which he lifts out. He removes the lid to reveal a delicious smelling something, yellow and bubbling. He ladles some into a bowl and hands it to me. I almost drop it – it is red hot!

'What is this? Magic?' I ask.

'Bean stew,' laughs Rufus as he ladles more into a bowl for Granpa and into one for himself.

Granpa sniffs and a grin breaks over his wrinkled face. I follow suit; it does smell delicious! My stomach growls and Rufus laughs,

'It sounds like your belly is less cautious than you are, young lady. Eat.'

But Granpa, too, is curious. 'What is this Rufus? You have no fire – yet you have cooked beans?'

'Sun magic,' says Rufus. 'I've seen the sun warm things

before it sets fire to them so I thought why not try catching it in my little cookbox here?'

I lick a little off the spoon. It is hot but, to my surprise, it doesn't burn me. I swallow a spoonful and a delicious glow goes right through my body, unlike anything I'd ever known before. The taste on my tongue is earthy, thick and nourishing. It's as if my body is being fed for the very first time. I eat another spoonful, and another, while Rufus talks.

'It was an accident at first. I left a dish of vegetables covered with a sheet of glass to keep the animals off and it started to cook. So I played around. This is much easier to hide when the guards are coming than a wood fire – there is no flame. The King might argue it's still fire but I say they have to catch me at it first.'

It tastes so great I'm eating more and more, faster and faster.

'Hey, Azra, slow down, you'll give yourself indigestion.'

I pause, the bowl is almost empty and I can sense he is right; I can feel my stomach protesting.

A bird hops up to me. It's so black that its feathers glisten. It cocks its head on one side and looks at me with its bright black eye ringed with amber.

'What is that?' I ask.

'A blackbird,' Rufus replies. 'They were bred in the palace aviary until someone opened the cage. Now a few still survive here.'

The blackbird comes right up to me, cocks its head as if to make sure I am still watching, then hops round in a circle before flying up to the top of a tree. There it sings, opening its golden beak to pour its tiny heart out into the most beautiful song I have ever heard.

Granpa stops and listens, his face softens as the pain of the past days lifts and, with my belly full of warm food, I feel a satisfaction I've not known before.

'It doesn't feel discontented here,' I announce.

They look at me, puzzled.

'This is supposed to be The Forest of Discontent,' I continue.

'I suppose there are degrees of discontent,' says Peter. 'I'm quite content with my lot, and so is our little songbird friend, but your aunt isn't.' He looks at Granpa, 'I suppose that is why you've come here?'

Granpa nods. 'I hoped you might know where she is.'

'I do – but I don't know if she'll see you.'

'It's not me that needs to see her, it's the child. I need to do right by the child. Will you take us to her?'

I jump up, clenching my fists. 'I'm not invisible! 'I am HERE, Granpa. Stop talking in riddles. What do you mean by *'do right by me?'* What you are planning?'

'We're going to see your Aunt Constance, that's the plan.'

I am so angry I could explode but Rufus interrupts.

'I'll take you,' he says.

He whistles and a golden-feathered Saluki hound appears, accompanied by a very regal-looking Siamese cat. I gasp at the sight of such beautiful animals. I have seen pictures but never believed they could look so glorious – and, like that, my anger fades as I focus on them. The cat is like a puff of smoke, her face etched in with charcoal.

'Stay! Guard!' Rufus says and the cat jumps up to the window ledge, erect, on guard.

'Come,' he says and the dog immediately follows at his heel, his feathers flowing behind as he strides forward, as do we, into the deepest part of the forest.

We start out along a well-used track but Rufus turns aside and starts hacking through the undergrowth. 'We'll take a short-cut,' he tells us.

We follow, the three of us hacking away, although I feel I am making no difference, just getting hotter and sweatier. I seem to spend more time trying to swat flies away than I do cutting. The flies get worse and worse. Then we come across the reason – the rotting carcase of a deer. The animal is half-eaten.

I have to walk by it and, as I do, I can't stop myself glancing down. I see its eye, glazed and lifeless. It's horrible!

'It's the way of the world,' Rufus says as he carries on hacking a way through. I shudder and, for an instant, my mind flashes back to that day, the day when my memory begins. The blood pounds in my head and all I can see is red.

I fall but I never land. Rufus catches me and, when I come around, I find that I'm strapped onto his back and he and Granpa are still hacking their way through the forest.

My stomach feels as if it has been pummelled and the movement, the rhythm of Peter's legs and the swinging of his arms, makes me giddy. I'm trying to speak, telling him to put me down, but the words won't come out. I feel as if the world is moving in a weird way. The green canopy can't protect me from the heat; it feels as if the desert sun is piercing right through the trees into my body, burning me up.

I have no idea how long we carry on in this way but, at last, we come to open sky and they put me down. I can barely stand on my own two feet. Groggily, I try to take it all in.

In Lady Constance's Caravan

In a clearing at the edge of the wood there's a bright yellow caravan on wheels standing in the shade. It's conspicuous against the green – but against the desert sand it would be invisible.

We are half way across the clearing when a woman appears at the caravan door. She is a strange sight, this tall, stooping woman dressed in what looks like expensive rags.

Next to her, Granpa is a wizened old man. The realisation shocks me, to me he has always been the figure of authority and the rock I relied on. He holds out a trembling hand, pointing in my direction and says, 'It's up to you now, Constance. It's your turn. It's time you took responsibility for what you've done. Here, ch...' For the first time he stops himself from calling me *child*, '…Azra, this is your Aunt Constance.'

I start trembling the minute I see this woman. I recognise her straight away – this is the witch who cursed Prince Sam, she is the one in the story, and Granpa is saying that this is my aunt? I feel like a parcel brought for inspection. She looks at me with no affection or interest whatsoever then steps aside and indicates we should go in.

My legs give way so Rufus scoops me up and carries me up the steps of the caravan, much to my embarrassment, into a tiny room with a curved ceiling. I feel paralysed and am trembling and cold. Is this witchcraft?

'Lie her on the bed,' she says. She bends over me and I feel her hand cool against my forehead.

I try but cannot turn my head.

'She has a fever.'

'Lies, all lies!' I try to shout it but my voice is stuck in my throat. 'I am not feverish.' I want to tell them. 'I'm cold, cold as the grave'.

I throw up violently and she's there with a bowl and catches it. Her sleeve brushes my face and the dark green velvet feels like moss. The woody smell of *oud* drifts from her and there must be some kind of magic in it because it soothes me.

She retreats to the back of the caravan, moving easily in the tiny kitchen, and makes a concoction, mixing and grinding spices and herbs which she bids me sip.

I protest. I don't want to drink anything she has had a hand in making but Rufus helps her make me swallow it. It tastes fresh and salty at the same time and cools my fevered body to the point where I recover enough to stop trembling and can watch and listen.

'The child is in shock. It's stupid to bring her here. It's dangerous for anyone to be found with me, but for her...'

She doesn't need to finish; I can feel the danger hanging over me in her unspoken words.

'It's time for you to take responsibility for what you have done.'

'What *I* have done!' Her voice rises and rattles the glass ornaments that festoon the van. She paces the tiny caravan. The anger sparks in her eyes as she turns on Granpa. 'You, my own father, have not spoken or been near me since before she...' – her finger points, quivering with rage, directly at me – '...

was born. I withdrew from my family to protect you all as much as I could. So how dare you come here and insult me by saying that *I* need to take responsibility. Where were you when I needed you? When the entire court turned against me? If you had been more of a father to me when I was humiliated then none of this might have happened.'

I have no idea what is going on and my head can't take it in. All I have are questions, the same ones that I've been asking all my life, and this isn't helping. It's raising more questions than it answers.

Granpa puts his head in his hands and weeps. Constance softens and she stops shouting and pacing. She sits down. Granpa is still sobbing until she reaches out her hand and touches his arm.

'Does she have the mark?' she asks.

He nods. 'At the back of her neck.'

She lifts my hair. I want to know what they can see but I still feel paralysed. She moves her hands down my limbs. 'She is in paralytic shock.'

'Have you ever seen the birthmark on your neck?' she asks me.

She reads the '*no*' in my eyes. She takes a mirror off the shelf and another from the wall and gives one of them to Rufus. She lifts my hair so, for the first time, I see it – a flame-shaped mark just like the one on the cover of *The Dragon Keeper's Handbook*. I've had this all my life – *and no-one told me.*

She retreats once more to the shelves in the corner of the caravan and mixes another potion. They feed it to me and I feel it slipping into my system, taking me into oblivion – and I welcome it. Just as I am drifting, Granpa comes and takes my hand and kisses it then kisses me on the forehead. I might have taken more note if I had known then that I might not see him again for many, many years, but it does not cross my mind that this man, who had tucked me into bed every night, would disappear so quietly and suddenly from my life.

So it comes about that I am left with this woman, Lady Constance Mackenzie. I don't want to call her 'Aunt' because I blame her too much for the troubles in our land, no matter what she might say.

There is only one bed, or so I think, but the caravan is built in the style of the old tinkers, so she tells me, and the reason the bed is so high is that there is a truckle bed on runners that pulls out at night. Rufus lifts me into it and then he, too, takes his leave.

So I go from sleeping under the stars on the roof in a bed-tent to sleeping beneath Lady Constance, the witch. I know I was in hiding in the city but I was so used to that, I had forgotten to be afraid. I tell myself I should be afraid of her yet, for some strange reason, I am not.

As I'm drifting off to sleep I remember my backpack. Even though I am still angry that Granpa hid the dragon's egg in my bed, I feel protective of it and worry that the egg isn't warm enough. So I ask Constance for my backpack and I sleep curled around it. I am not afraid of her but I don't trust her and I don't want her to know my secret.

I wake at first light and lie thinking over all that has happened. I feel, with my fingers, the birthmark on my neck. Now I know that it is there, my fingers can trace the slight difference in texture and I remember when I was young that I could feel it changing – a hot, burning sensation when danger was near. I am uncertain about this woman but, if I can rely on my birthmark, it is neutral with her.

She pulls the truckle bed right out and stands with a spatula in her hand. I'm shivering again.

'You look as if you could do with a hot meal. Have you ever had a hot breakfast?'

'Oh, yes. Gramma always made rock bread and stone-fried eggs.'

'Ah, yes, 'Gramma' would find a way round anything. But I'm talking of porridge.'

'I'm not sure. I don't know what it is. And how will you cook it?'

'Rufus made me a sunbox cooker, right here in the kitchen.'

She hands me the warm bowl of strange stuff and pours honey on it. I lift the spoon to my lips and the smooth porridge stuff slips down, almost liquid but not quite, and oh so sweet from the honey. But, best of all, it warms me in a way I had never believed possible, right down to my toes. I wriggle them.

But is this what witches do? I suddenly remember the fairy tales Granpa used to tell me. They feed you good things, get you to like them, then... what do they do then? I can't quite remember. I have to watch out. But Granpa brought me here and he said I would be safe here. Safe? How can I be safe in the hands of a witch? But I don't say it.

I decide it will be easier to run away from this witch's caravan than from Granpa – not that I'd ever tried – because I can see that she doesn't want me here and I don't want to be here either. So I reason that I can sneak off and live in the woods. But first I need to get my strength back.

Constance begins to look different to me. At first she looked sort of like the illustrations in *The Handbook* –

white-haired, clad in rich, dark silks and velvets. In the book she had looked old, crooked and wizened, her hand crabbed like a claw, but now I can see she isn't as old as I'd thought. In the story, I thought she was as old as Gramma and Granpa but, of course, I now know she is their daughter. I wonder if *The Handbook* will tell me more but I am too weak to read at the moment.

I throw up again but this time she isn't quick enough so it goes in my hair and all over the bed. She has to strip the bed and wash my hair. She mutters under her breath, 'Take responsibility. *Setdamn!* Why does he think I live like this? Stupid old man! Comes here without a word of comfort for me after all these years.'

'Why should he comfort you? You are the one who cursed the King and the Prince

– and, in doing so, you cursed us all.'

'You don't know even the half of it!'

I can see that I've touched a nerve and I am pleased. I hate her going round looking after me, behaving as if she is my mother or Gramma.

'You say that the whole court turned against you but you cursed the Prince. Why would Granpa support you in that?'

'That wasn't when the court turned against me. They did that long before, through no fault of mine. And your grandfather let them. It's an old story and one I have never spoken of.'

She continues to dry my hair and brush it and, as she takes care of me, something in her changes. It's as if she softens. I feel her taking her time, lingering over brushing my hair. I shrug her off, impatient.

'Ah, you've your mother's temperament!'

I think that is the end of the matter and then she turns and looks down her long nose at me.

'Well, as you have read what others have said of me, perhaps now is the time to tell my version of events, or at least some of it.'

Lady Constance's Story.

'When I was young, the world was a very different place. There was peace in Set. We were open to the whole world and traders came from the four corners of the earth and they would come to the court and the court was buzzing. We had great parties and celebrations. I wore great silk and satin gowns and your mother and I would help each other dress for the grand occasions.'

Her eyes light up as she talks and I enjoy hearing of my mother in this way. It feels strange to hear of her talked of like this. I've never really heard about this part of her life; all she talked of when I was small was what was happening around us. She never talked of the past. I assumed it was too dark and terrible to hear but now I realise it was because it was an easier time. It feels good picturing her having fun.

'My father, your Granpa, was head of the Mackenzie clan through his mother's line. The Mackenzie clan was the closest to the King. Apart from members of the royal household, only the Mackenzies had unannounced access to the King and your grandfather was Jonas Mackenzie Seth, Lord of the Flame.

I interrupt her, 'Lord of the Flame? What is that?'

'He was in charge of all the Fire Ceremonies – the great displays that took place throughout the year to celebrate the dragons – and any rites of passage such as births, marriages, coming of age, deaths.

I stop her again, 'So was he a Dragon Keeper?'

'No, it is his great disappointment that he was not. Dragon Keepers are born, not made. It has to be inherited but it is not necessarily passed on. It may skip a generation or two – and it passed him by. The passing of the Dragon Flame from father or mother to son or daughter is almost as mysterious as the art of Dragon Keeping itself. Some say that Dragon Keepers can be trained, and your Granpa was one of these, but they have limitations – one of the most important of which is that they cannot access *The Dragon Keeper's Handbook.*'

'But he did!' I exclaim as I bounce up and down with delight and I tell her of how the book came to life for Granpa.

She gives a wry, pleased smile. 'That must have pleased him greatly. They always said he was one of the greatest not born to the art.'

'So why wasn't he killed?'

'Chancellor Vlast saved him.'

'Chancellor Vlast? Who is he?'

'He is the King's brother. He has the ear of the King and he also speaks for the King. He is in charge of the Palace Guard and the security of Set. He has helped me so much. He is the only one who ever came to see me after...' My aunt looks around the tiny caravan and now I can see it through her eyes; she has made this small space comfortable but for her it is still a prison, an exile from the family, friends and life she once knew. She sighs, then continues, 'Chancellor Vlast persuaded the King that it was a greater punishment for your Granpa to be declared a fraud, as he was not a true-born Dragon Keeper – which he had never claimed to be. It was now made illegal for him to be Lord of the Flames and he was stripped of his titles. Vlast said that his humiliation was his punishment. It was made worse for him that I was publicly shamed.

Her robes rustle as she moves slightly, as if to distance herself from me, before she continues, 'But that was nothing to when the Dragon Keepers were outlawed and first your father and then your mother were…' She hesitates as if gathering the strength to bring out the word, '…killed.'

The way she said that, that one word, I saw how much she loved my mother. Yet something puzzles me.

'How do you know this? You said you had not seen Granpa since I was born.'

'Vlast told me. He is my only link with the old days, him and Rufus. And Vlast was right, it is a far greater punishment than death – the humiliation and sorrow robbed your Granpa of all his strength.'

I am confused. 'You talk of this Vlast as if he is a friend. How can he be a friend when he did all this?' I ask.

'He did it to save our lives, your Granpa's and mine.'

But all I can think is – he didn't save my mother.

She looks out of the window but it doesn't look as if she is seeing anything.

'In the years when the dragons were held in high regard, the ceremonies were fantastic and, after the King, your Granpa was the most important man at court. He was in charge of all the Fire Ceremonies, the great court displays of fire-spinning, fireworks, fire-breathing and dancing.' Her voice is bright and light as she paints me a vivid picture of the gaiety of those times. 'Did you know your Gramma was renowned as the best fire-dancer ever to have danced at court?'

'Granpa told me.'

'And your Granpa honed his fire-breathing skills by playing the bagpipes?'

'The *bagpipes?*' I burst out in disbelief.

'Yes. Didn't you know? Bagpipe playing and fire-breathing complement each other.'

'I never heard him.'

'No, the pipes were outlawed.'

I hardly recognise Gramma and Granpa in these stories – so much that they had done when they were younger is now illegal.

'I was to be betrothed to the King. We grew up together and were so in love that it was plain to see. He was older than me so he had to wait for me to come of age but we had known for some years that this was to be.'

I look at her, wondering if this is true or is she living in her own fantasy world? She lifts up her right hand and a ruby ring on her finger flashes its red light around the caravan.

'When Chancellor Vlast found this Dragon's Eye Ruby, the King immediately had it made into a ring as a gift for my sixteenth birthday. It was to be our engagement ring. We were not able to announce our engagement publicly until I reached twenty-one so, until then, I wore it on my right hand.'

She starts to cry and I am wondering if this story may

have tipped the balance. Is she sane? It would be no surprise to me if she were not for she has gone from being the sure-to-be Queen to living like a gypsy – the reverse of the fairy story. No-one ever tells you what the ending is for that story but I'm sure it's not happy.

'It was the great Midsummer's Eve Party and, as my birthday was on the 21st of June, it was decided that was to be the night when our engagement was announced. Officially, only our families knew...' She hesitates and I see something of the young girl in her, remembering a time when life was so very different. 'We danced and danced – and we had eyes only for each other. Then the fire display began – and something happened. I don't know what but, before, everything was fine, normal, as usual, and after it...' She stares

down at her ring and it is as if
the light has gone out of both it
and her. The tears pour down
her cheeks. 'Afterwards he
didn't come near me, didn't
look at me. He only had eyes
for her...'

We sit for so long in
silence that, at last, I can wait
no longer. 'Who? Who was
she?'

'She was Sheikha Esther,
the leader of the Dryseas tribe.
She had been captured when he
conquered the Dryseas. I
befriended her and she had
heard me talk of nothing but
him. She knew of our promise.
She knew we loved each other
and yet she...' Constance looks
at her ring as if she is watching
the scene playing out in it.

I sense the deep sadness
in her.

'That night, at dinner,
she raised her goblet to toast
him and he responded by

raising his. They drank a toast to each other and, from that moment, he never looked at me again. He only had eyes for her.' She tears her gaze from her ring and looks directly at me, her eyes full with the hurt that still courses through her veins.

'When I tried to confront him he had me forcibly removed from the court. I became a laughing stock, a source of ridicule. I was mocked openly; children would pelt me with rotten tomatoes and not once, *not once* did my father speak up for me.'

If it wasn't for the sincerity of the woman in front of me I don't think I would believe this. Why would the King do such a thing? I wonder what the true story is.

'Overnight, I went from being the King's beloved and a favourite of the court to being shunned, a pariah, pointed at and whispered about in the street. The city was a terrible place for me, humiliating, so I came here and took refuge in the forest. Rufus made me this caravan. If ever I need to disappear I just drive into the desert and the caravan disappears into the colours of the desert sands.'

She pauses and her hands caress the wood of this home that Rufus has built her, this beautiful wood with every corner carved and shaped so lovingly. It's a home fit for a queen, but a gipsy queen, forced to roam in her mobile prison.

'I didn't dream of returning to court but after the birth of the Prince, when the Queen died, Chancellor Vlast came and invited me to the christening. He said things had changed. I couldn't resist. I thought, *hoped* that King Qahir's feelings for me had somehow returned. I had this idea, this belief that the spark of love was still there, that I could go back and become a mother to this motherless Prince and rekindle the love that had been so cruelly denied me. I still felt this love so strongly for both of us, so surely it was possible to reignite it in him again?'

I can feel her looking to me for support, for an answer that I can't give her.

'But you *cursed* the Prince!'

'Says who?' demands Constance.

'It's written...'

'You should beware of believing everything you read. Books are just one person's view of the world.'

I remember my mother tearing a schoolbook from my hands, telling me the same thing, 'You shouldn't believe everything that you read; it's just an opinion. You need to weigh up the facts for yourself, look for the truth.' But what of *The Handbook?*

Constance continues pacing the room, talking passionately, and I can tell it is the first time she has let herself talk of this.

'I'm a seer. I *prophesied* the Prince's future. I told them what I saw so they could watch over him, take precautions.'

'Ban fire?'

She shakes her head. 'No, no! I knew that would do no good at all. It is the Prince that needs protecting. This has just made the people miserable. It's killed the life force in the kingdom; there is no love any more – it is the King that has turned it into a curse.'

I hear her almost choke on the bitter words, that the

man she loved could do such a thing. Listening to her, I think that her love isn't in the past tense, she still loves this man and I begin to believe her story. She has talked so long, sitting in the pitch dark, that my eyes have grown accustomed to the shadowy room. She reaches out to me and her hands rest on the backpack on my lap. I sense that she can feel the egg. Her hands explore the shape and I pull the bag towards me, protectively.

'What is in here, Azra?'

I know that I need to trust her, that she is the only one who can help me.

'It's an egg.'

Her hands move away and I can tell that she has guessed. 'A dragon's egg?'

'I have to hatch it.'

'How?'

'That is what I have to find out. I have to bring dragons back to the world.'

'That is why your Granpa brought you here?' She paces the floor, thinking. I can't tell at first what her mood is but, when she speaks, I hear the fear and excitement in her voice, 'You will need fire. Do you know how...?'

I shake my head.

'I can show you how to make fire, that much I know, but you have to find out the how.'

I feel as if I'm being whirled along at high speed and halted on the edge of a precipice. I've been given a job that's way out of my league and now this woman can teach me the first step – but, for the next step, I need to step off the edge. Perplexed, I snuggle the backpack with the egg under the duvet with me. My mind is in a spin with everything I've been told – and I feel afraid of what is expected of me.

I lie awake for hours, my thoughts in turmoil. I have come to realise how twisted the tales have become, the stories of my parents and of the Dragon Keepers are distorted to give a sinister view of their lives and deeds but with just enough truth to make it difficult to argue against. Granpa may have kept me hidden but, until I was eight, I had seen and heard what everyone thought of them – of us. Now I know I'm not just the child of Dragon Keepers, *I* am a Dragon Keeper.

And I know what they do to Dragon Keepers.

And what of my aunt? Is she a Dragon Keeper too? She sensed the egg straight away. If so, why can't she hatch the egg? Everything I've learnt over the past few days has led me to believe my mother was the last. But then, until yesterday, I didn't even know I had an aunt.

Once again it occurs to me, if I'm not supposed to believe everything I read, what about *The Dragon Keeper's Handbook*? If my aunt isn't a Dragon Keeper, how can she help me to hatch the dragon? I don't see any resemblance to my mother in this bitter woman but neither does she seem to be the evil witch who cursed Prince Sam either. All around me, the silence of the forest. Silence so powerful I can feel it. It creeps into the tiny caravan and envelops me, dense and dark, like some strange blanket. I sense it as a kind of fear creeping over me. Then, just as it becomes almost unbearable, a noise – the cry of a Night Owl – sweeps into the room, a Nightjar *kroo kroo kroos* across the desert and I tell myself what my mother used to tell me, 'It's only the dark; dark never hurt anyone.' I fall asleep, my mind full of darting birds of prey which turn into dragons and my aunt flies with them, her multi-layered clothes forming great wings as she glides through the air. And so I fall asleep.

To my surprise, I wake at dawn and pull *The Handbook* out of my backpack. A sunbeam stretches across the floor and reaches my bed as I move *The Handbook* out of the shadows into its spotlight:

The Dragon Keeper's Handbook

'A true Dragon Keeper is born – they are set apart by the Flamemark, a flame-shaped birthmark that is the sign of one singled out by the Dragons. Only they possess the innate magical powers with which they can access The Dragon Keeper's Handbook and can be a true Dracoman – one who can speak Draco, the Dragons' own tongue, without any teaching.*

After the Dragon Wars, the term Dracoman became an insult and meant someone with a serpent's tongue, not to be trusted.

Acquisitors *are not true Dragon Keepers but persons who have learnt the skills of Dragon's Breath and other* *esoteric arts.* **To be an Acquisitor** *was a mark of honour – until the time of the Dragon Wars when the term became one of abuse and an insult. They were even rarer than Dragon Keepers, these Acquisitors, and were carefully chosen by the Dragons and taught a Keeper's skills in times of need.'*

So what is my aunt? She doesn't seem to fit any of these categories but then, neither do I. They say that I am a Dragon Keeper, which means I should have innate knowledge, but I certainly can't speak *Draco* and I've no idea how to hatch a dragon's egg...

Crime and Punishment

The sound of hooves echoes around the palace courtyards as the Prince rides through on his stallion. The old palace meat wagon stands by the cellar door. He barely notices it until a shoe flies through the air and startles his horse, Fakhr al Badiah. He turns and sees Lords Pacatore and Vruntled, the latter only wearing one shoe, being bundled into the back of the wagon. More curious still is the fact that the King is watching the proceedings.

He turns to the King. 'Father, where are Lords Vruntled and Pacatore going?'

'The Dryseas,' the King says as he turns away.

Shocked, the Prince asks, 'Why?'

'That is Palace business and no concern of yours.'

'Father, I'm not a child. When I succeed to the throne...'

'If...boy, if. Nothing is certain in this world.'

'I need to know what is going on. All I have learnt are skills that any good soldier would learn but with the affairs of the court I am in the dark. '

'Now is not the time.'

Until now, Prince Samardashee, or Prince Sam as he was known to his intimates, has usually been obedient and loyal to his father, doing as his father bids him, but this day something snaps. As he takes hold of his stallion he mutters, 'Today may not be the time for you but it is the time for me!' As he swings into the saddle, his anger and determination fuel him. 'Come!' he commands his horse but the King seizes the reins.

'Get down, boy!'

When the Prince refuses, the King takes his sword and slashes the girth strap, unseating the Prince. Chancellor Vlast and the Captain of the Guard are watching and smile to themselves as Prince Sam carries his saddle to the stables and the King hands the stallion to the stable hand.

'No more riding for the Prince today.' Then had the Prince escorted to his room.

But the Prince is no longer a child and times are changing. The King rules with the weight of his fist and his crown, Prince Sam wins people over with his kindness. What the King does not know is that the Prince and the stable hand are friends. This friendship is secret because the Prince was kept from playing with other children who the King saw as beneath him.

But the Prince and Jasper, the stable boy, became firm friends with their shared passion for horses. When the Prince quizzed him on his name – an unusual choice as it means *Master of the Treasure* – he was both surprised and delighted when Jasper told him his father, the head groom, called him that because he regarded the horses as treasure and hoped his son would also.

As soon as the coast is clear, Jasper saddles the Prince's horse. This horse is the Prince's pride and joy. It was his mother's horse and named Fakhr al Badiah, *Pride of the Desert*. His name was not just because of his magnificent looks, this horse was at home in the *Dryseas* and able to survive and track it like no other. With Fakhr al Badiah positioned below his window, the Prince immediately appears at Jasper's call and leaps into the saddle.

He rides at speed, swiftly covering the ground between the palace and the Forest of Discontent but, as he rides along the edge of the great wood, a sight meets his eye that fills him with despondency. A *djin,* or dust devil, has blown up. The tiny sand pillar, less than 3 feet in diameter, whirls across the desert sands, lifting the trail of hoofprints and wheel tracks that Sam is following up into its midst, whisking it off in a swirling column high into the atmosphere.

His heart sinks. Dismounting, he scans the ground. The tracks have gone. What can he do? He pulls his scarf tighter around his face and the scent of cloves and chewing tobacco fills his nostrils for it was only last week that the always generous Lord Pacatore gave him this as a gift when Sam admired it. He smiles and removes the scarf.

He holds the scarf out for Fakhr al Badiah, whose nose twitches as he inhales Lord Pacatore's distinctive smells. The horse's large nostrils are more sensitive than a dog's. He moves a step, stops. His nostrils quiver, sniff the ground then up high in the air. He moves forward a couple of paces then stops once more, sniffs and now he has it. Sam leaps into the saddle, pulling his *keffiyah* around his face and they speed off. With the forest a green blur on his right, the swift-footed Fakhr al Badiah covers the distance fast. They swerve right into the vast open space of the desert and they are, at last, beyond the effect of the sandstorm and Sam can see the tracks once more. But, more than this, he can see the meat wagon in the distance. He urges Fakhr al Badiah towards it but the horse refuses. Carefully, Sam tries to turn the horse once more. Again Fakhr al Badiah refuses. Sam knows his horse too well to insist. He gives him his head and they continue along the trail of the outbound tracks while the meat wagon appears to be driving back in the direction of the palace.

Now Sam sees the reason why – two figures, one tall and stick-like and the other round and short, have been abandoned and stand some distance from the retreating wagon.

He stares in amazement and halts after the hard ride to water both himself and his horse now his goal is in sight. 'He's put them out to die in the Dryseas? Why would he do such a thing?'

Playing With Fire

Constance presents me with a cup of herb tea and fresh fruit with the dew still on it. Her talking bird squawks, 'Eat up! Eat up!' every time I pause.

The drink is so hot I can't touch it and I find it so strange, this e x p e r i e n c e o f h e a t . Mesmerised, I watch the steam rise from it. To me, it's like a magic that has been there all my life, within my grasp yet I have been unable to reach out and touch it.

'If that hot drink is fascinating you then you've a lot to learn. You don't even know the basics. Have you read anything about how to hatch a dragon's egg?' Constance demands.

'No. There is nothing in *The Handbook.*'

'Then even *The Handbook* doesn't think you're ready for this and time is running out.'

'Running out?'

'It's the Prince's sixteenth birthday tomorrow.'

I think to myself, 'And mine.' I wonder if she knows that – but there are more urgent things to consider.

'That is when it happens,' says Constance

'The prophecy?'

'Yes, no matter what the King thinks, *he* can't change destiny. Only a dragon has the magic for that.' She storms out, her great cloak sweeping *The Handbook* off the bed as she goes. I want to burst into tears. How am I supposed to know what to do?

The book ripples open, the pages flowing like water – and I see it – the book is open at an illustration. Now it's not just a great screed of tedious history; these are paintings showing a girl, not just any girl, but it looks just like *me*! And she/I am doing those stupid tricks my Granpa taught me: taking a mouthful of water and spraying it out – all the different ways of doing it. I slump, disappointed, with *The Handbook* in my hands.

When Constance returns, I'm still sitting there, miserable.

'It's no good! There's nothing in there – just the stuff Granpa used to make me do with water.'

She turns the book around and looks puzzled at the open pages. 'Blank,' she says.

'Can't you see it?' I ask, disappointed. I think I was half expecting her to be a Dragon Keeper, this confirms for me that she isn't. I can see the pictures clearly and, even though she has turned the book around, they are still the right way up for me, but for her the pages are blank.

I seize the book from her. Then it hits me like a blow to the head. This book is for me, no-one else; it is telling me how *I* can do it. I know Granpa kept saying this to me but now I *feel it*. Now I *know* what it means.

I look at the pages again. I try flicking through to see if there is any more information but they won't turn. Then I notice that beneath each illustration are figures:

1-0 x 10 +1 60s rep x 60

I have no idea what the figures mean but I am pretty sure that *The Handbook* wants me to practise water spraying. That must be what I am ready for so that is what I will do.

Constance watches me closely as I take a jug of water

and a glass outside. It is a long time since I last practised. I had a big row with Granpa, saying that I was too old for these games but he'd insisted.

At the first attempt I choke and the water runs down my chin. Constance stands watching at the top of the caravan steps.

'What on earth are you doing child? We don't have time for you to mess around like this.'

Does she think I don't know? I am so furious the water explodes out of my mouth as I turn on her. 'This is what *The Handbook* is telling me to do.'

My outburst ejects the water farther than I've done before. The sensation ripples through me, the explosion of energy.

'That's better,' Constance tells me. 'You need to project it farther or you will burn your face.'

'This is water!' I tell her.

'You don't think they use *fire* when they start teaching fire breathing!'

And, at last, I get it! Granpa had been training me in fire breathing in the traditional way after all.

I repeat it, remembering how it felt, the surge as I project the spray. This time it is even better; there is no dribbling and the spray projects a good three feet into the air with no splash back. But I know I need to be consistent. Granpa had insisted on it. I start counting how many I can do in succession. After an hour I can do ten in a row without any spillage.

Suddenly, I know what the figures in *The Handbook* mean. I seize the book –

1-0 x 10 +1 60s rep x 60

Excitedly, I read out the calculations, 'Ten short, sharp, focussed sprays followed by one long spray, all done within 60 seconds, repeated consistently for an hour.'

A whole hour?

I look up at Constance as I tell her, 'I know how to hatch the egg.' As I explain, I see the fear in her eyes. As I talk, *The Handbook* turns more pages. Aunt Constance can see the book's pages turning. It stops, revealing the next step to me. I rest my hand on the page under the heading:

The Dragon's Breath

I read aloud, ' *The Dragon's Breath* is the technique handed to human

Dragon Keepers in sacred trust from the ancient dragons. '

Now it's not me, but Constance that has cold feet. 'You can't do this Azra. Your Granpa was foolish to think it is possible. Even if you can do the fire breathing it is too much to expect of you.'

She comes down the steps, wrapping her long robes around her. She looks into my eyes and I can see she is genuinely worried and afraid for me.

To my surprise, I feel quite calm. 'Granpa taught me. You said yourself that he was the best and he told me that he had taught me everything he knew.'

'What *he* knew. He wasn't a Dragon Keeper. He didn't know the Dragon's Breath – that is the stuff of legends. You can get seriously hurt, or worse.'

She isn't joking – *The Handbook* has some pretty horrific illustrations of what can go wrong. Luckily, she can't see any of those.

'How do you know all this?'

'Because your mother and I were close. I watched her training and she confided in me. The Dragon's Breath was the stuff of legends. I'm sure even she didn't know it.'

I glance at the illustrations and one turns and it's my mother – with her scarred lip angry and blistered. I shudder as I realise this is a fire-breathing scar! Something puzzles me, 'So why did Granpa teach it me?'

'Your Granpa was disturbed by your mother's death. He couldn't face it and, for him, it was made worse by the fact that she was the last of the Dragon Keepers. For him that meant the death of hope.'

'Granpa believes I'm a Dragon Keeper.' I say defiantly.

'A Dragon Keeper needs to be trained, to bring out that innate knowledge in them. Even if, by some miracle, you did do it, a dragon grows quickly and what if it turned on you?'

Then I see that it is Constance who is afraid because it is beyond her knowledge. But I have the knowing of it, a knowledge deeper than anything I've been taught. Besides, it isn't just me, *The Handbook* is telling me what I need to know. Granpa only taught me the basics – this is all he knew. *The Dragon's Breath* sets out how to hatch a dragon's egg. One hour of structured breathing, I thought, was a challenge – to actually hatch a dragon's egg, *The Handbook* tells me, can take anything from a few hours to days. My fear is of failing – but I know this is what I am meant to do. Any shred of doubt I have is removed when I hear my mother's voice, telling me clearly,

'You have to bring the dragons back.'

'If you can give me fire I can do this. Look, I've not spilt a single drop in the last hour of practice.'

She shakes her head. 'Playing with *water*! Look at how mesmerised you were with a hot drink! Fire is totally different – it's dangerous - and from what I've just seen you'll never master it.'

I challenge her, '*You're* afraid because *you* can't do

this! You don't know how to make fire!'

'I know how to make fire, Azra, have no fear. But teaching it to you is another matter. This whole thing is too dangerous.'

'If you won't teach me then I will find out somehow.' And she knows I mean it.

'It's not just that,' she continues. 'When a dragon emerges from its shell, whoever it sees first it adopts as its parent. The bond is unbreakable. Only a dragon can bond with a dragon. Only a dragon *should* bond with a dragon. It's a terrible responsibility and it's too much for you. It's too much for anyone. No human has ever bonded with a dragon before.'

That, I did not know. So maybe her real fear is that I will succeed.

The Dragon Keeper's Handbook

The Dryseas

'The Arab traders who used to come to Set were in awe of the vast desert lands surrounding the Kingdom and gave them the name of *The Dryseas* for, to them, it had the questionable honour of being the driest *erg* or sand-sea. Within living memory there had been the remains of a once vast landlocked sea but that is long gone. The desert winds here come every 30 days, blasting away any drop of moisture in the atmosphere and reaching speeds of up to 50 miles an hour, sculpting great waves of sand dunes in this ever-changing landscape. Not a single tree or bush grows here. The very air sucks the moisture and life out of your body. You can feel it happening the moment you step onto the desiccating heat of its sands.'

In this endless sand-sea, the only sign of life is the meat wagon wending its way back across the barren waste to the palace, having deposited its cargo.

Lords Vruntled and Pacatore stagger in the parched heat. They move because they have to – standing on the sand is torture; walking, the lesser of two evils, is only agony. The guard who brought them here took pity on them. He would not leave them water for that would only prolong their agonising demise.

The blazing sun beats down on the desert landscape – thousands of miles of dry, barren sand and wind-blasted stone stretching beyond the eye of man, a seemingly infinite wasteland.

In the dry silence of the desert their two voices start a barrage of complaints and whining until they become too parched to speak. Lord Pacatore sits down on the sand, takes out his kerchief and tucks it into his collar. He then starts reaching out and looks as though he is eating and drinking. He calls out happily to Lord Vruntled, 'Come, join me!'

Lord Vruntled turns and sees his companion, still sitting, miming eating. He watches a moment then stumbles back through the sand towards him and shakes him by the shoulder.

'You great buffoon, what are you playing at?'

The shaking of his shoulder brings Lord Pacatore back to the harsh reality of the hot, dry desert. Lord Pacatore's lip quivers, 'Where is it? The food, the wine?' he bleats.

Vruntled croaks very deliberately and very slowly, 'It – was – a – mirage.'

Lord Pacatore doesn't want to believe this. He looks around at the unforgiving desert and he definitely does NOT want to be here. He keeps looking and looking, searching. In the distance he hears Lord Vruntled's voice echoing, the mournful sound of desolation and pessimism – but it's too far off, it doesn't penetrate for Lord Pacatore has seen something else.

'Look!' He points a pudgy finger still, in *his* mind, greasy from the fatty chicken he holds and, his speech slurred with the imagined wine that flavours his palate, says, 'It's moving. It's coming towards us. Look!' He points, and keeps pointing, his finger quivering with insistence that there is something there.

Vruntled can't see whatever Pacatore thinks is there. 'There's nothing there. It's just another mirage.'

But there is still hope in Pacatore's eyes. He sees a way out, fuelled by the food that he has just envisioned.

Vruntled shades his eyes and gazes, still unseeing. 'It's hopeless!' he declares.

Still Pacatore points with a focus and determination that he has never shown before in the face of his friend's doom and gloom. It is at this moment of crisis that Lord Henry Pacatore, descendant of a long line of noble Pacatores and, until now, the one who stood out only as the black sheep of the family, is now the one who stands out as the visionary, the saviour of the moment. This moment is redefining him; he is the only one who can see, the only one who believes. He can see their future, and it is coming to rescue them.

Pacatore stands, his barrel of a body staggering a moment until he finds a firm foothold. He steadies himself and now, rock solid, waves his arms in victory in the air.

Vruntled, in despair, falls to the ground. 'I thought there was nothing worse than a fool, but there is – a fool with visions.'

Lord Pacatore, to Lord Vruntled's amazement, finds a strength in the blistering heat that enables him to stand steadfast, his arms still held unwavering up in the air. Then

Vruntled hears him exclaim with gratitude, 'My Prince!'

Vruntled opens his eyes and groans at what he sees, 'God make my end swift. I, too, see the mirage.'

The Prince recognises the distress of the old courtiers who have been like grandfathers to him. He dismounts from his stallion and gives Vruntled a sip of water and slips a pebble into his mouth to help him salivate. His words tumble around the pebble. 'Thith ith worsth than I feared; thith ith desthert madnessth.' Lord Vruntled would have wept if his tear ducts had allowed.

'Save your strength. Do not speak,' the Prince tells him.

Vruntled tries to babble on but the Prince silences him.

'For once, my friend, keep your mouth shut if you want to survive,' the Prince tells him as he ties his spare *keffiyah* around Vruntled's head and mouth and carefully wets it from his water bottle. The sun is tormenting him and he can see that the two Lords, woefully out of condition, are reaching a critical stage. 'We need to get out of this sun.'

He helps the two men onto his horse. They sit back-to-back and slump, voiceless at last, while Prince Sam leads the horse gently but firmly. The hot sand is burning even through his soldiers' boots. He knows that for every hot, aching move that he makes these old men would feel it tenfold and the thought that he can do this for his old friends comforts him.

Every few minutes he plies them with water until, to his relief, they resume their usual banter. At first they are full of effusive thanks for the privilege and honour of riding on the Prince's horse and they even offer to change places with the Prince. But, after a few hours, they regain enough strength to start their bickering. In spite of the heat and the sweat, the Prince smiles to hear them up to their old ways.

Lord Pacatore complains, 'I don't like travelling backwards. It doesn't suit me. Why do I have to travel backwards?'

'Because you are watching our backs.'

'Well, there's no-one there.'

'Good. They are keeping away because you are watching our backs.'

This pacifies Lord Pacatore for a while. Then Lord Vruntled takes his turn.

As the complaining rumble between them grows the Prince asks, 'The King said that he was sending you on Palace business?'

'Of course, of course,' nods Lord Vruntled.

'But I didn't believe him.'

'You didn't?' says Lord Pacatore in surprise.

'Whenever my father tells a lie his left eye twitches. That is why I came to find you – and to find out why he banished you.'

'Oh your father didn't *banish* us. As if...' but the Prince interrupts Lord Vruntled before he can conjure up more words.

'Why else would he have you driven out to the Dryseas and dumped you here to die?'

Lord Vruntled does not want to go into this. This is territory that could lead him, or more likely the bumbling ramblings of Pacatore, to reveal The Secret. The Secret that has been kept from the Prince since the day of his Naming. The Secret that has changed the face and fate of the Kingdom of Set. The Secret that no-one even dare think of, never mind name. The Secret that has kept this young Prince an innocent boy. The Secret that Lord Vruntled is determined will not pass either his or Lord Pacatore's lips.

Lord Vruntled feels Lord Pacatore's substantial rump squirming behind him and he knows his old friend well enough to realise that he is struggling to keep The Secret. Lord Vruntled, a master of distraction, looks around and, to his relief and surprise, sees the answer.

'Ah, look, the Forest of Discontent!'

Pacatore becomes even more agitated and restless, trying to squirm around in the saddle to see, but in vain. Then, at last, he comes up with a solution; he bends over the stallion's hindquarters and lifts up its tail to look between the horse's legs. He sees the forest.

'Hmm mumble de Didimomten!' He almost chokes in his excitement, turning bright red and purple at the sight of the green, vibrant trees that mark the end of the monotonous sight of seemingly endless sand.

Lord Vruntled turns, wondering at the gobbledygook his friend is spouting. As he turns, he feels the stallion's belly distend and sees Pacatore, head down over the horse's arse. Lord Vruntled feels his legs stretching apart as the bloating in the stallion's stomach becomes more and more urgent. Vruntled shouts a warning, but too late! The massive fart explodes out of the horse's rear into the reddened face of Pacatore. The full force of the blast hits him in the face and he bounces in the saddle, his ceremonial dirk stabbing the horse in the flank. It rears up, tearing the reins out of the Prince's hand, and takes off with the pair of lords hanging on for dear life. The Prince can only stand in astonishment, watching as they disappear into the depths of the forest. Their cries of panic resounding above the sound of hooves.

The Dragon's Breath

Constance calls me. 'Help me with this,' she demands.

She wants me to help her move a large tarpaulin covered in leaves and insects that looks as though it hasn't been touched in years. Reluctantly, I help her haul it back to reveal a great pile of wood.

'This is Rufus's store of apple wood from when the old orchard died,' she tells me. 'He kept it aside as it is a very special wood; it burns slower and hotter and has flames the colour of the rainbow.'

My sullenness and anger at her turns to interest as it dawns on me that she's going to help me.

'So you *do* know about fire?'

'Of course, I was a fire-dancer! Some say I was

destined to be greater than your Gramma. That wasn't to be the case but your Gramma taught me. And, as a fire-dancer, I learnt all there was to know about fire. This wood is what we need for the dragon's egg to hatch; it's slower to catch fire but, once it does, it burns hotter and it will entice the dragon with its scent.'

'Really?'

'Dragons have a very highly developed sense of smell.'

'How come you know about dragons?'

'I worked with your mother when she was training. As a fire-dancer I helped her to learn all the different types of flames and she taught me things about dragons.'

It is strange to think of her and my mother growing up together and, again, I feel how much I miss my mother. 'It must have been really nice having a sister to grow up with.'

A smile turns up the corners of her mouth. 'Yes, it was.'

She cranks up the handle of the little chimney that is usually hidden, tucked away on the roof of the caravan, and opens the doors of what I thought was a corner cupboard to reveal that it is a stove. It's beautiful to watch her creating the fire.

She takes a piece of wood and makes a tiny hollow in it; around this she carefully places a few dried leaves. Then she takes a knife and shaves tiny curls of dried wood onto them and crumbles dried seed heads and grass stems into a fine powder. Over this, she strikes two pieces of bright steel that glisten in the sunlight and, as she strikes them, a spark flies. It darts as fast as a firefly and just as quickly it disappears. At the third strike the spark lights the powdered wood and seeds and the leaves catch fire.

I watch the magic, hardly daring to breathe. The flame goes out. As Constance sits back on her heels I cry out, 'Let me try!' I seize the fire steel from her and, after one or two disappointing attempts, I get the hang of it and the dried shavings and leaves ignite.

Soon we have a great blaze going – and it is the most fantastic thing I have ever *ever* seen. I watch the great leaping yellow flames devouring the wood, fascinated. But I get too close and the heat is *unbelievable* – it feels like the sun has fallen into this tiny hearth. No wonder the King is so afraid of it.

'Look,' Constance says, 'can you see the pictures?'

I look into the flames and pictures appear like figures from the past. Is that my mother? At first it makes me sad and then it gives me courage. If I can make a fire, I know I can do the *Dragon's Breath.*

As Constance feeds the flames, I take the dragon's egg and hold it gently.

Constance talks as she works, the long stored memories from her youth, 'I seem to remember that dragons check on their young, that they are still alive and healthy in their shells, by breathing fire on them. That makes the shell translucent and they can see how the baby is doing.'

I grab *The Handbook* and open it – and there is a new page.

The Dragon Keeper's Handbook
How to Take Care of a Dragon Egg

When water spills on a Dragon Egg it changes colour. The Egg becomes an iridescent rainbow of fast-changing colours and this is the warning system for the Dragon Mother that she needs to move her Eggs to safety fast.

Water can change the temperature of the Egg and if it gets too cold the Embryo Dragon will die.

'But how do I hatch it?' I want to cry with frustration.

Constance urges me, 'Read on.'

*The shell is so solid it can withstand the shock of earthquakes and volcanic eruptions for this is its natural environment – to be born and incubated in the heat of the volcano. But it still needs to be handled with care. A Dragon Egg is a magical, precious thing and many things may disturb the Embryo Dragon, hence the saying from Settlers of old: '***Let sleeping Dragons lie***.' Once it is woken, it will start to hatch so the time needs to be right. A Dragon Embryo can survive incredible catastrophes yet it also can be unsettled or de-formed by the slightest thing. To ensure a perfectly-formed dragon the temperature needs to be kept constant, ideally at the Nest temperature of the volcano.*

'It must be dead! My bed was never the temperature of a volcano!' I throw the book aside in disgust. How do they expect me to do this? In spite of all I've said I feel like a child. I feel fear grip me. I'm not ready for this and I want to lay the blame elsewhere.

Constance picks it up again and hands it to me. 'Now look here! I knew your mother better than anyone and she would never have endangered a dragon. She must have known something, had some reason for keeping the dragon's egg with you. Maybe it just needs the high temperature to hatch.'

'Huh, as if! With me and my amazing *Dragon Breath* technique, some chance it's going to have.'

But she opens the book and hands it to me.

The Dragon Keeper's
Handbook
Dragon's Breath

A Human has never successfully used The Dragon's Breath to hatch a Dragon's Egg and we do not want you to use it, young Azra...

I stop reading. My name dances and sparkles before my eyes *AZRA* it's as if it's in giant letters – now this is personal. This is for me.

...because it is so dangerous – but we see that it is the only way.
      Your Mother was teaching herself this – she was

just as stubborn as you and it is her picture, not yours, that we show in The Handbook. You have not earned your place in here yet.

Your Mother used to practise in secret but her Father found out and helped her develop her skills. His love for her gave him a skill beyond that of the usual Acquisitor.

So he taught her, first with water then with fire – the same skills that he taught you, young Azra.

Now you have to play with fire – and this is what gave your mother the scar on her mouth. A careless mistake, one moment without focus and you can burn your face off.

So beware, young Azra – for you ARE playing with fire.

As I read this out to Constance her attitude changes, 'If *The Handbook* says you can do it then it must be true.'

'It doesn't say that, it says that it's the only way.'

'Then I'll help to keep you safe. I was there when your mother was burned. That is why the scarring was so slight – and I have some lotions in case of emergency.'

She lines up bottles of lavender oil and aloe vera and fills jugs with water from the well in the clearing. I touch my lip, feeling the lines of it, and remember my mother's scarred lip. She never would tell me how she had got it; just that it was a burn.

Great! Constance knows how to treat me if I burn my face but I don't want to get burnt so I make up my mind. As Granpa said, 'If you think you can do it, or you think you can't – you're probably right. Whatever you decide is what will happen.' So I picture myself making the perfect flame for the *Dragon's Breath*.

In the book there is an illustration of the bottle of liquid, purple and translucent, and a jar of white powder, just the same as those Granpa Jonas gave me, so I find them in my backpack and start the process.

Constance hands me a lighted spill and, as I breathe out, I ignite my breath and direct it onto the egg and it glows. The glowing egg reveals a shadow within. I breathe on it again and the egg becomes more translucent and the shadow takes shape. The egg now seems so fragile. It looks just like a stone in daylight but its colour changes in the firelight, becoming almost translucent, revealing the delicate life within. I feel my heart pounding as I see the tiny dragon shape within its shell. Is it alive?

'How can I tell if it's alive?'

Constance looks and I see she, too, is astonished at the wonderful sight – the tiny foetus curled within the stone-like shell.

'Look, there's its claws!'

'And that's its wing folded over...'

'...its head!'

'And there is its tail!'

We exclaim at every detail we decipher – but we still can't tell if it is alive.

I stop in wonder – but Constance reminds me I need to follow the sequences in *The Handbook*. The view of the dragon within the egg is just what I need to go on. My heart is racing – but is the tiny creature alive? I can see it but, as yet, it hasn't moved.

I keep the *Dragon Breath* going – counting, breathing, focussing. Constance keeps the fire burning, handing me a fresh flame for each breath. We work and the sweat trickles down my forehead so Constance ties a scarf around my head. My shirt is sticking to my back and the tiny caravan is unbearably hot but I have to keep going – for once we have started we cannot stop. *The Handbook* is clear on that; once the process of *The Dragon's Breath* is begun it must be completed. I can see why no-one has succeeded before, the sequences of one hour fire breathing are gruelling. I had felt daunted at the prospect of an hour but *The Handbook* tells of hatchings lasting for days. I dare not think of that; all I can do is focus on each breath, each sequence. I don't count the sequences or the hours, I just do it. On and on we work and the breath and the flame flow out of me – but still nothing happens.

I look at Constance, sweat pouring from me. I'm covered in dirt from the smoke.

'One more time,' is all she says.

My lungs ache; they feel like they could burst. I close my eyes and wish from the bottom of my soul as I breathe with what feels like my last breath. It comes up from deep inside me, my face and lips burning hot – my last *Dragon's Breath*.

For me, there is nothing but the fire, the flame and the egg. I hear a voice announce, 'For too long the Dragon Keepers have hidden the dragons. Now it is time for the dragons to reveal themselves, to come out of their shells into the light. I am Azra, Queen of the Dragons, and I will help you, take you back to your rightful place as guardians of the gems... the stones that warm, colour and reflect in your dragon wings...the emerald, ruby and turquoise that shimmer in your scales... the glorious colours formed from the heat in the heart of the earth and that pulse through your dragon veins and feed the flames that blast from your incredible mouths – the tongues of fire that create and destroy – for in your power and magic is all that is needed to save the Kingdom and the Earth. Peace will return to the land and the Kingdom of Set will be a great and beautiful place once more, reunited with the rest of the world.'

From a long way off I hear Constance's voice calling me, 'Azra, come back! You must come back!'

For a moment I'm stunned; I don't know where I am. I realise with a shock that these words are from *my* mouth. Constance smiles at me and in that smile I see my mother looking at me.

'Well, Azra, I think you are a child no more. You are a woman and a force to be reckoned with.'

There is a cracking sound and we both look down to see that the egg is beginning to open, the crack wide enough to reveal the movement of a tiny elbow. The splintering egg yields to the force as the dark purple dragon's wing begins to emerge.

We look at each other and I see in the aloof Lady Constance Mackenzie's eyes something I had not anticipated – respect.

Night in the Forest of Discontent

The Prince follows the trail into the woods but, as darkness falls, there is still no sign of the missing Lords. Worse still, he has returned to the marker he left earlier and he realises that he is lost. Frustrated, he wraps himself in his cloak and settles down for the night. He has thought of only the two desperate Lords. Not for one moment has he considered his own needs – and now he is exhausted, hungry and thirsty. The only one of these he can satisfy is the exhaustion so he makes himself as comfortable as he can on the hard, unforgiving ground and falls into a fitful sleep.

Something wakes him. It takes him a while to get used to the strange light in the wood.

The moon is high so that even in the gloomy forest he can make out the shapes of the trees – but there is another light, a golden glow that isn't from the night sky. It's a light coming from the earth and there is a sound, a crackling that he does not recognise. He draws his sword and, cautiously, makes towards it.

He sees a strange hut-shape and out of it shoot yellow ribbons of light, bright as the sun. He draws nearer and feels heat coming from the crackling, sparking tongues of light. His heart beats faster for there is only one thing that he knows of that can make this strong, hot sunlight on earth. They say that they are all dead but he is not so sure.

In all the stories they tell of him they say how brave he was for killing the last dragon but he did not feel brave. For he was three and all he remembers was putting his tiny pinpoint of a sword into the already dying dragon and he remembers the resistance – the hard, unyielding scales. Then his uncle showed him the soft spot, the only vulnerable point on a dragon – its eyes. His Uncle Vlast lifted his sword arm and the dragon looked straight at him and it stopped struggling and surrendered to the young Prince. His sword pierced the dark pool at the centre of the green-gold eye and the life went out of it. He still remembers that eye. He has never, in his heart of hearts, believed that all the dragons are dead; that one blow of his tiny sword could extinguish the might of the dragons – and now he is going to find out.

He moves, cautiously, towards the light and the fire – for that is what it is – roars as its flames shoot into the night sky. The roar confirms in his mind his suspicions, and he realises that his father was right when he stressed the need to be vigilant for here is a dragon when they had thought that all were slain.

He mounts the stairs to the dragon's lair and, as he draws his sword, he kicks open the door.

The sight horrifies him. Two women are kneeling before the fiery beast. All he can see is flames – and a young girl has fire spewing from her mouth.

"Fear not, I'll save you!' he yells as he bounds forwards and hurls the old woman to safety. As he turns back, the young girl clutches at his arm, yelling, 'No!'

He pulls her aside but, as he looks, he sees there is no body to this beast, just a fiery mouth. Then his eyes fall onto the thing on the hearth. It looks like a stone but, emerging from it, is a creature that is changing colour as it comes into the light. Its green-blue scales look soft, its tiny claw clutches onto the edge of the shell. It draws its head out and looks up, opens its eyes and he stops and they look straight into each other's eyes.

But the Prince has no time to do more for, at this second, Lady Constance Mackenzie hits him over the head with the shovel and, with a groan, he collapses to the floor, unconscious.

I pick up the newly-hatched dragon and look into its eyes but it gives a terrible mewling cry and starts looking around. It sees the unconscious boy on the floor and its cries redouble.

I look at Constance in horror.

'It's too late! It has bonded with the Prince!' she says.

'The Prince! How do you know it is him?'

Constance points to the royal insignia on his sword.

I cry out in frustration, 'What can we do now?'

The seconds tick by as we both focus on the unconscious Prince and the distressed dragon. As the moments pass, a wind blows up through the open door, rattling the ornaments and making the flames roar. As the wind passes, *The Handbook's* pages flick open, riffling through the whole book until, at last, the wind dies down and the pages come to rest. I stare at it.

'What is it? What can you see?' demands Constance.

'It's only a map. I don't see what good a map is to us.'

But Constance thinks differently. 'A map of what?'

I squint at the book which is sideways on to me. 'It's a map to the Dragons' Nest, the old volcano,' I read.

Constance is pacing up and down – as much as you can in a caravan this small with an unconscious prince lying in the way. 'It's the perfect hiding place. Take the dragon there. No-one will think of looking there. It's under the Palace and right under their noses.'

'But what about the Prince?'

'I will deal with him.'

The way she says this worries me. 'Promise me you won't kill him.'

My concern surprises me but I've always felt the Prince

had a rough deal with this prophecy/curse thing. 'It looks like he was trying to save us when he burst in – that's what he cried out. And his reward is to be knocked out.'

She seems taken aback that the thought she might kill him should have entered my mind but I still don't know how much to trust her.

'I promise.' She sees that I'm still mistrustful. 'I'll give him something to make him forget tonight for at least the next twenty-four hours and I'll give him something to occupy his mind – with luck it will erase the memory permanently.

The dragon is now out of its shell and flies with unsteady hops, jumping out of reach every time we attempt to catch it. It jumps onto the Prince's chest, mewling and flapping its wings. The Prince groans and opens his eyes. It's only for a second but the look is one of mutual respect and it seems to settle the dragon. Then the Prince lapses back into unconsciousness.

I take the broken shell and persuade the dragon to eat it. It feasts on it eagerly and, sated, it, too, falls asleep – on the Prince's chest.

I look down on the Prince – and here, in the midst of it all, I see this young man who has been the focus of so much of my emotional turmoil. It is him who I've blamed for everything that was wrong in my life. Because of him there is no magic in the land. Because of him there is no fire. Because of him I had to leave school – though maybe I should forgive him that because I hated school anyway. But, most of all, because of him my parents were killed.

Yet, somehow, over the years, I felt a growing empathy for him, how he, too, had a raw deal through no fault of his own. Now I see just a young boy, turning into a man, and he tried to save me, fool that he is. If I'm honest, I like the look of him and, you have to admit, I hadn't had much of a birthday and, from the look of him, he hadn't been doing any celebrating either.

I feel my hardened heart crack open inside me but time is ticking and I need to get away from this prince because, if he is to forget last night, I don't want to be there to remind him of it.

I make a travelling nest from my backpack and place the sleeping dragon inside it – and wonder what am I to do when it wakes.

Constance reads my mind. She eases the Prince onto

the bed and removes his shirt and cape and hands them to me.

'Wear these.'

I don't want to.

She pushes them into my hands and explains, 'They smell of him. The dragon might take some comfort in that when it wakes.'

I realise it's a good idea and dress in the Prince's clothes. He's bigger than me, the cape swamps me but I like the feel of it. I like the smell of it. As I head out of the door I glance back and see the half-naked Prince lying on the bed and I blush.

Constance gives me a worried look, 'What is it?'

'Nothing.' I say this yet it doesn't feel like nothing to me – inside, I feel a connection, a stirring I've never felt before but I don't want to admit this, certainly not to Constance. I cover, I hope, by adding, 'They'll be looking for him.'

'That's why you must go.'

The Prophecy Realised

The Prince wakes to the smell of something delicious, a smell like he's never known before. He touches his head and finds that it is bandaged and groans. He has no idea where he is. He looks around and can barely take it in. He is in a strange bed in a wooden hut but where?

He tries to dredge up the memories of last night, a confusion of images: bright light, dark, hunger, exhaustion are all that come to him.

An old woman approaches him and makes him drink. He resists at first but she insists, 'You've had a shock. Come, this will make you better.'

He drinks and, as the liquid eases its way into his system, the haze of last night becomes even hazier.

'Where am I?'

'You are in the Forest of Discontent. You stumbled upon my humble caravan last night when you were exhausted and delirious.'

He glances down at his half-clad body. 'Where are my clothes?'

'Who knows, Your Highness?'

He looks up when she calls him that, confused, but that strikes home.'

'That I do remember. I am Prince Samardashee. But how did you know that?'

She indicates the sword with the royal insignia emblazoned on it.

He struggles to remember last night but what little there was is completely driven out of his head when he sees the old woman turning a spit over a sun-like thing – hot and bright. It moves! It lives!

He pulls himself upright, backing into the corner.

'What is that?'

'It's a fire, Your Highness.'

'Fire?' The Prince is curious. Something is tugging at his memory. There is something – but still he cannot remember. 'What kind of magic is this fire?'

'Ah, have you never seen a fire before? It looks like magic but it's something very practical. I use it to cook food.'

So saying, she breaks off a chicken leg and hands it to the Prince on a plate. He picks it up and instantly drops it. 'It's HOT!'

She laughs, 'Yes! So you've never had hot food? Taste this, it's chicken.'

'Chicken? Those little things that lay eggs?' He looks at it in disbelief. 'It smells good.'

He's still hesitating so she tears the other leg off the chicken and starts eating it herself. Tentatively, he takes a bite. The juices run down his chin and the flavour explodes in his mouth. His eyes light up in delight.

'This,' he announces, 'is delicious! In fact, it's the best thing I have ever tasted in my whole life!'

He devours the chicken leg and, before he has finished, she has replenished his plate with more and has given him bread to mop up the juices. While he's eating, she joints the rest of the chicken and, that too, the ravenous Prince eats, eagerly. He gives a loud burp as he finishes and smiles.

'This,' he says, pointing a chicken bone towards the fire, 'is the most miraculous thing *ever.* It gives off heat as strong as the sun and transforms food into something *exquisite.*'

Constance bows her head in acknowledgement.

'You must come with me and bring this magic to the palace.'

'Ah, I can't do that, Your Royal Highness. The palace is no place for me, a simple woodswoman. I am not fit to appear before the King.'

The Prince is about to command her to obey but she is too quick for him.

'Besides, wouldn't it be more fitting for Your Royal Highness to take this amazing gift to the King? I can show you how to feed it, carry it and spin it.'

Fitting her actions to the words, she picks up a staff and descends the caravan steps. She lights both ends and there, in the dark of the forest, she spins the fire – a show of such beauty that the Prince is mesmerised.

'That is the most beautiful thing ever – these little flaming suns here on earth. Wow! It's… it's…' He is at a loss for words.

He seizes the stick to try spinning for himself but Constance refuses, insisting that, first, he must learn about fire – how to make it, to respect it and how to put it out. Throughout the day and well into the night she trains him.

The heat makes the sweat pour down his naked torso. He should be exhausted but the adrenalin and excitement drive him on. He will not give up. However, he becomes exhausted and weary. He becomes clumsy and he burns his hand. At this point he wants to give up. Constance makes to walk away but he stops her and persuades her he will go on.

She bandages his hand and then relights the fire spinner – which he now sees is no ordinary staff.

She spins it and then hands it to him. 'Now you are ready.'

To his amazement he can do it. He spends the next two hours doing tricks and swirls, beats, waves and butterflies. She teaches him well. She watches carefully. Now his head is so full of the beauty and mastery of fire that when the potion wears off she is certain he will have replaced the memories of last night with this.

She fashions him a torch of ripped hessian, soaked in tree sap and bound around a branch. 'Now you can take this to your father.'

'What if it goes out?'

She looks at the youth and feels a glow in her heart.

These hours together have been the happiest she has spent in years. He reminds her of his father and the love that still is within her. It softens her and she surprises herself when she hears herself saying,

'This flame is like love; to keep it alive you have to pass it on. Each time it burns low, take a new branch, pass the flame on and it will keep burning.'

They see the light of the dawn spreading across the treetops so Constance points him towards his home.

'Just keep the sun to your right and you will be heading due north to the palace,' Constance tells him. She watches as he sets off eagerly, running with a steady, easy, loping stride, his flaming torch held high.

As the Prince runs it's as if he is transformed from a boy

into a man. With each stride his strength grows, each bead of sweat on his body washes away the overprotected boy that his father has raised. His muscles pop and groan and he revels in the sheer physicality of it. As the path becomes more overgrown, he slashes his way through with his sword, the blood pumping through his veins strengthening his resolve. The thorns catch and tear at his breeches but he takes no note of this. He must get back before the brand dies out. He is not sure that the old woman is right, that he can pass the flame on so easily and he watches it anxiously as he runs. Pieces of hessian sap-soaked rag fly off but he knows no other way to preserve it than to run – fast.

He reaches the edge of the forest and pauses for breath, never so joyful as he is now to see the palace stretching its great walls out before him. To him, they look like welcoming a r m s . T h e b r a n d i s uncomfortably hot now that it has burnt down. He sees the sign that reads *Forest of Discontent* and laughs at it. 'Not for me,' he says as he slashes the '*Dis*' off with his sword so it now reads '*Forest of content*'. He picks up the slashed finger from the signpost and binds it to the old brand, giving him a longer handle.

Setting off again at a steady pace, he wonders if they will be watching out for him. He anticipates the surprise, the honour with which they will greet him, bringing this incrediblc gift for them.

To his surprise, a squirrel jumps down and follows him. He kicks at a rat at his feet but it just skitters a few feet away and then returns. He chases it a second time but still it follows him at a more discrete distance so he lets it stay. Birds are wheeling overhead and he smiles at this escort heralding his return. The sun is rising and the heat from it and the heat from the burning torch make him sweat more with each step he takes – but it is really of no matter to him for he can see his goal, the palace, his home, just ahead.

The sweat blurs his vision and the heat haze makes it worse but he can see movement along the palace walls. The palace parapets are lined with courtiers and soldiers. His heart jumps.

'They're watching out for me!'

He is so thrilled to see them that he pushes himself forward, ignoring the ache in his limbs and the heat that threatens to overwhelm him. When he sees the sunlight glinting off his father's crown he feels a thrill. 'At last,' he tells himself, 'he will be proud of me. He will see that I, Samardashee, am a man.'

But, as he draws near, he sees the gates remain closed.

'They don't recognise me,' he laughs. He look down at his bare, sweating torso, streaked with black from the smoke. Such a contrast to his normal courtly attire. He calls up, 'Open the gates! It is I, Prince Samardashee. Look what I bring! I bring you a great magic, a great science. I bring you FIRE!'

But the gates remain closed and he can hear the rumble of displeasure and disbelief.

'Sire, it is me, your son. Do you not know me? I bring to you this great gift of fire!' Prince Samardashee kneels and bows before his father standing on the castle parapet.

The King can contain himself no longer. 'Look what you've done! Just look!' the King roars at him.

Prince Samardashee's gaze follows the pointing finger back to where he has just come from. To his horror, he sees that the forest is ablaze, engulfed in fire, the animals fleeing from the blaze. Stunned, he drops the burning brand at his feet and the straw-strewn drawbridge catches alight. Panic ensues and the crowd start calling out,

'It's the curse! The curse!'

The gates open and the guards emerge, stamping at the flames, but to no avail.

'Water! Get water!' yells the King, who is now on the drawbridge and comes, unheeding, through the flames.

A guard seizes a jar of water from a nearby cart and tips the liquid onto the flames but they shoot higher.

The guards start hosing the flames with water from the moat, trying to douse the flames on the drawbridge. However, nothing can quench the anger that is raging through the King.

Chancellor Vlast, his dark smile hidden beneath his beard, takes advantage of the confusion and the King's loss of control. Vlast turns to redirect the Palace guard – unbeknown to Qahir and Samardashee – sending them inside the walls towards the newest part of the Palace – before declaring, 'Why, what witchcraft is this? Fire that burns more fiercely with water? This is the dark arts, sire. None since the ancient Byzantines knew this secret.'

The King makes his way towards his son. 'You fool! You ignorant fool! I've done everything, *everything* to protect you from this and still you...'

The Prince stands firm and, at first, it looks as though the King will strike him down. 'What are you talking about? Protecting me? From what?'

'From fire!' the King yells. 'At your birth, an old witch foretold that you would destroy the palace – and me – with fire.'

Never has the Prince faced up to his father like this but he is also his father's son and the anger is also part of his make-up. He explodes with the wrath of one who has been over-protected and lied to and had things hidden from him his whole life, 'If I'm ignorant, it's you that has made me so. You aren't protecting me, you're protecting yourself!'

The King thunders, 'It's the same thing! If I hadn't been here to protect you, you wouldn't have lived to inherit.'

If Prince Samardashee had turned his head to look at his uncle he might have had some inkling of the future but Samardashee is focussed on the fight between himself and his father and misses the glowering look of hatred that Vlast throws towards his brother. A stranger would wonder how the King had survived his brother's jealousy, living in such close proximity – but that tale, of a mother's love for her two sons, is for another time.

Vlast clenches his fist at this. If *he* had been king, oh, how different this kingdom would be!

The Prince is raging too, 'What do I want with a palace?

I want to travel the world, to seek adventure, not be stuck behind these dark, gloomy walls for the rest of my life.'

'This is the world – there is no other world but this.'

'Then, if this is it, I don't want it.'

At one stroke, the Prince has just destroyed the King's whole reason for living. The King lurches towards him and Prince Samardashee thinks he's going to hit him but it's the King's heart stopping in his chest that makes him stagger. He falls onto the Prince who throws the old man off and draws his sword. At first, he doesn't understand that his father is dying and still rages at him, 'You knew! All this time you knew and you kept it from me.'

The King, red-faced, falls to his knees, his sword the only thing that is keeping him upright – and then the Prince knows. He bends down on one knee.

'Father?'

That one word is enough. There is loving kindness in that word and the King's hardened heart expands and bursts with love, exploding in his chest, released from the fetters that have kept it imprisoned all these years. The release is too much for his body; this body that has defeated a pair of oxen in a trial of strength and slain the finest warriors to grace the battlefield is unable to withstand the power of allowing the love into his life that he has denied for so many years. He looks at his son with a tenderness his son has never seen before.

'I only did it for you, my boy, only for you.'

Before Samardashee's eyes, the King transforms from

the colossus that led armies into a vulnerable old man – and the Prince sees that his father is dying. All the hurt, hatred and resentment disappear as his love for his father takes over – and he weeps. The tears soften the old King's heart even more and the bitterness that has tainted his love disappears. All that is left is a father's love for his son. This is the legacy he leaves.

Through the smoke of the burning palace, the spirit of the Queen appears and, for the first and last time, the Prince sees his mother. She bends over the King and he kisses her with his last breath. He smiles, a smile of pure love and joy. His spirit leaves him and stands hand in hand with the Queen and they smile at their son.

'Don't worry my child. This was prophesised when you were born. Your father tried to prevent it but sometimes we just have to accept our fate.'

She leans forward to kiss him and a soft, sweet breeze brushes his cheek. He touches his cheek but all that is left is the memory of the kiss. H e opens his eyes and all around him is chaos and confusion. He inhales and the choking smoke makes him gag. His father lies l i f e l e s s   i n   h i s   a r m s. Immediately, his Uncle Vlast is there, ready. He removes the crown from the King and he raises it up to place it upon his own head. However, two hands, strong and cool as they touch his, also take hold of the crown.

Vlast looks up in anger and astonishment. Who dares to defy his authority? His eyes meet the eyes of the Syed, the tall, venerable leader of their faith. He drops his gaze in recognition that it is the Church that crowns the new king. Vlast drops to his knees in acknowledgement of that, fully expecting to be crowned.

The Syed takes the crown and, above all the din, his voice rings out, 'The King is dead! Long live the King!'

Vlast waits in vain. He looks up and, to his fury, he sees that the Syed has placed the crown on the kneeling Samardashee.

The Syed continues, 'King of the Settlers and the Dryseas.'

Everyone falls to their knees in deference to their new ruler. Vlast tastes the bitter gall in his mouth, the taste he knows of old when, for the first time, he realised that, as the younger son, he would never be king while his brother lived; how he has striven and schemed over the years and never succeeded in what he thought was the simple task of getting rid of this boy. But now, surely, it is his right to be king until the boy reaches manhood?

King Samardashee is stunned for an instant and Vlast recognises this and seizes the moment. 'This is too much, Syed, for the boy. It is all right, Samardashee. I can take charge.'

But with the crown and the death of his father comes something that Vlast had not foreseen in Samardashee – a strength and an anger. His anger is twofold: that he, Samardashee, is responsible for his father's death and, secondly, that all around him at court had known the prophecy and hidden it from him; these people that he has known all his life, that he has grown up with. He sees soldiers he has played and trained with. He scans the battlements and hears the screams. He sees the courtiers leaping to the safety of the waters of the moat and he is afraid for them. He feels responsible for them and he makes a vow. 'There is no need, Uncle.' He turns to the crowd, aware that mere moments ago they were so hostile towards him. Now they are in shock. Their kneeling and accepting of him as king is a knee-jerk response to the Syed. Samardashee sees this and he knows he has to handle this well.

'My people, we will be avenged for this! This witch will answer for this terrible day. But now we must fight this beast, this fire that my father has protected us all from. We will fight and we will conquer it.'

Vlast glowers. This is not the boy that he has manipulated and coerced and fed with fears and doubts. Where has this new king come from? This does not fit in with his plans. He renews the vow that he made when the Prince was born – the vow that this new boy-king has to be destroyed, one way or another.

The Hunt Is On

King Samardashee is as good as his word. His days hanging around the palace with the older courtiers have taught him who is the most knowledgeable and who to trust. His Uncle Vlast has miscalculated this boy who was so silent which Vlast mistook for passivity, this boy who had been watching and observing without judgement.

King Samardashee takes charge. He seeks out the Earl of Settle who is responsible for the management of the Forest of Discontent.

'Earl Settle,' King Samardashee asks as the elderly Earl bows, 'I remember you saying you fought forest fires in your youth?'

'Aye, sire, but I have never seen this fire that thrives

when water is poured upon it. I have only heard tales...'

Vlast has no patience for this. 'Sire,' he says, the word sticking in his throat, mentally reaffirming his vow that Samardashee must die and not just die but be dishonoured and his memory destroyed so that all that is left is shame. From this, the glory of Vlast's rule will rise. 'Leave this old fool to his reminiscences. We must go.'

'Patience, Uncle. A moment now may save many lives and help us overcome the fire.'

The Earl continues, 'I remember an old trader telling me there were three things that could work with what some called Greek fire...' He pauses, trying to remember and Samardashee waits, determined to be patient. '...sand works,' the Earl recalls.

They all look out towards the vast sands of the Dryseas – so much yet so far away. Samardashee shakes his head.

Vlast interrupts again for it's no help to his cause if Samardashee can quench the fire in the old palace. 'Sire, there is no time for this. We must flee the palace.'

But Samardashee ignores his uncle and waits patiently.

Lord Settle's rheumy old eyes water at the young King's consideration and patience. At last he remembers, '…and urine, sire. Yes, pissing on the fire can put it out.'

Vlast roars, 'What nonsense! We're not going to stand pissing onto that!' He points at the flames that have already devoured the drawbridge and the outer gates.

However, Samardashee has already moved on. There is no sign of the Palace Guard and there is no time to hunt for them. Samardashee organises men, women and children so that they are pissing into buckets to pass hand-by-hand up to the tower where the fire has not yet taken hold. They pour the piss on the fire and a small section of flame goes out – and stays out. A cheer goes up and they redouble their efforts when they see they can succeed.

Samardashee appoints Lord Settle in charge of this and organises the women and children – supplying them with drinking water and any containers they can piss in. Soon the chaos is more organised. The fire still rages around the moat, the drawbridge and gates are gone but the main palace is intact as the fire is halted with just the doors singed.

Satisfied that the fire is under control, King Samardashee selects six men and they head for the stables. There he stops for a moment – in the heat of the moment he had forgotten. He had forgotten that the last time he had seen his beloved horse it was racing into the forest. He turns to Jasper who is watching him uncertainly.

'I last saw Fakhr al Badiah racing into the forest with Lords Vruntled and Pacatore clinging onto him for dear life. I had hoped that he at least would return here.'

Jasper shakes his head.

'Is there any word of Lords Vruntled and Pacatore?' King Samardashee asks.

'None,' Jasper replies, 'And their names have been stricken.'

'Stricken!' Samardashee is furious. 'For why?'

The stable boy looks reluctant to tell so Samardashee beseeches him, 'Surely you can tell me, Jasper?'

This appeal as friend to friend carries more strength than any kingly command.

'For breaching the code.'

'What code?'

'Where none light fire for fear of fulfilling the prophecy.'

Samardashee looks in astonishment at Jasper. 'So I am not the only one to bring fire to the palace these days.'

'No...' Jasper hesitates then makes up his mind to tell all to his friend, the King. 'It is said that most of the palace used to eat at the Breakfast Club, that the Lords were the mere scapegoats. But, as a warning, their names were struck from the record so they no longer exist.'

'Then I will unstrike them!' Samardashee declares.

'That cannot be done!' Ochamore – a righteous and mighty warrior who had fought as Samardashee's father's right hand throughout all his campaigns – declares, then corrects himself, 'It has never been done.'

'Then I shall be the first to do it.'

While Samardashee speaks he saddles his father's horse, a magnificent black warhorse which the old king had favoured to bear him in battle. Each scar on this magnificent beast has a story to make your hair stand on end.

Then Samardashee leads the men and their horses into the courtyard as Vlast appears and insists on coming.

'No, Uncle Vlast, you are too invaluable here. I entrust the palace and my father's funeral preparations to your care.'

As Samardashee rides off, the indignity of being dictated to by this boy-king infuriates Vlast.

'Funeral preparations! Is that what he thinks I am fit for? That boy, who I have wiped the snot from his very face, has the cheek to dishonour me in front of my men! He has no idea who he is dealing with. I have been too soft, too patient. Now is the time and this throne, this Kingdom, this Crown, which by rights should be mine, *will* be mine.'

His wife turns to him and smiles her agreement. He tilts her face up towards his, 'And you, my love, will at long last be Queen.'

The King gallops towards the forest. The sun is still not at its zenith and the horses move easily in the coolness of the morning. As they reach the dark woods he leads them around the edge, travelling south speed, the less direct route but, on horseback, it will be quicker. He is not thinking; he is using his instinct, knowing she will have fled yet still he heads for the campsite where he left her. His instinct is that she will head for the desert, thinking he will believe she will go deeper into the forest. But it does not matter if he is right or wrong for he *will* find her. That much he knows – for he will not stop until he has.

The Seven Warriors

The caravan has gone, the tracks swept away, but Samardashee is no fool. His youth and lack of experience do not matter for he has spent his sixteen years well, observing those at court, seeing beyond the courtly manners and masks that all wear before the King. In those years the young boy saw what skills and passions those at court had, the things that kept them alive in spite of the times of cold and hardship.

One of these is Merilin, an archer who can hit a moving target at 20 paces – but that is not her main talent. As Court Hunter, she is another whose job has fallen out of use and favour but now he can put her skills to good use.

He halts them outside the clearing and bids Merilin to enter alone. A single set of tracks lead to the main path into the wood, the only path possible for the caravan to take. However, Merilin is not satisfied; she examines the whole clearing and then makes for the desert and bids them follow.

'You were right, sire. She has laid a false trail. If not for your instinct we might have fallen for it.'

Constance has half a day's head start on them but the caravan is heavy while they are light and their horses swift. She will be relying on the caravan being camouflaged in the desert sand, its colour blending into the landscape like a lizard's skin. But Merilin's real talent is more of a gift; her skill at tracking means she can decipher the tracks in the shifting sand and even over rock.

When Merilin finds faeces from Constance's horse, she turns with a grin. 'This is less than twenty minutes old. We've got her!

They scan the sand but, still, her caravan is invisible. They ride under Merilin's direction and it's not until they are almost on top of the caravan that they see it.

Young King Samardashee, eager for revenge, rides abreast the fleeing caravan and, as his horse pulls alongside Constance, he draws his sword.

In that instant, the sunlight reflects on his sword, blinding him for a moment and, at the same time, giving him a vision. He has a flash of recollection. The sun glints on the sword and the light illuminates a memory: this woman with a young girl – and the girl is breathing fire. The image is strong enough to pain him. He reels and lowers his sword.

'What have you done to me, witch?' he demands.

'I did nothing but help you fulfil your fate,' she retorts defiantly.

At this, he raises his sword and strikes but she shields herself with her staff and the sword hits her ring. The glistening ruby ring shatters into seven pieces, the light cascading off every surface and every shard finds a home in each of the warriors, each beam of light working its way into them and performing its magic, starting the process that will transform each recipient.

The shard that pierces the King enters his eye and now he has another flash, a vivid recollection of what happened that night. He roars – a mixture of anger and outrage. He wants to obliterate this memory but now that his eye has the clarity of vision from the ruby shard he cannot erase it. He turns on Constance in fury.

'A DRAGON! You hatched a dragon, old witch?'

The shockwave passes through the warriors; they are not prepared for that. Fear flickers through the group and the horses skitter at the sound.

'Aye, does that shock you Princeling?' But the proud old woman instantly regrets her arrogance, the trait that has always been her undoing. In those words of defiance she has given him the proof he needs, that those flashes are not mere imagination but the reality of that night that she had tried to erase forever from his memory.

Murray, the old sea-warrior, until the ruby shard

entered his heel, had long moved with a limp sustained in a battle injury that impeded him greatly. To his and everyone's surprise, it is the ancient Murray that leaps from this saddle and with a speed never witnessed before in him – old or young – he leaps into the driving seat and seizes the witch's horse, bringing the caravan to a halt.

Ochamore, the fiercest fighter in the land, strikes the old woman sideways off her seat and onto her knees. 'Kneel before your King.'

She hesitates before she looks up, 'King? You are King since dawn, Your Highness?'

'Thanks to your deceit and cunning, witch.' King Samardashee controls his emotions. He does not want to show his grief before this woman who has he knows not what power over him.

' Then King Qahir must be dead...'

Ochamore, to avoid more insolence, thrusts her head down so her words become a mouthful of dry sand and she chokes and splutters her grief and tears into the desert so none but she and the shifting sands know how deep it hurts. He looks to his King for the command to kill but Samardashee curbs his impulse for immediate revenge. This woman knows too much, and much that might be useful.

'Bind her,' King Samardashee commands. He watches her defiant eyes as he demands, 'Where is the girl?'

Her mouth may be stopped, dried up with sand, but her eyes betray the girl more than any words. Kneeling in the desert sand, Lady Constance Mackenzie sobs for the first time in almost twenty years with compassion for another human being, for the innocent niece whom she has failed so miserably to protect.

'Who is this girl?' As the King speaks, it's as if the warriors are waking.

Ochamore makes Constance rinse her mouth with water and sip – but this is no act of mercy or charity, it is purely practical – they need her to talk.

'Your name, witch?' But, as Ochamore looks into her face, he recognises her and says in his astonishment, 'Lady Constance Mackenzie!'

'Aye,' she speaks with humility for at last she recognises that pride, her downfall, does not serve her well and will not save her niece.

Then, Azi-Dhaka, the Dragon Slayer, steps forward. He pulls Constance's bowed head up by her hair. 'Sister of Agnes Jonas?'

'Aye.'

He turns to the King. 'In the Dragon Wars there were two Dragon Keepers who were the bane of my life. They were husband and wife: Arwin Nejem and Agnes Jonas, sister to this wretch. They had a boy-child but he was never found; a child born on this very day, sixteen years ago.

He holds his prisoner's hair tight and, all the while, he and the King watch this woman for every movement of her face, any flicker of emotion in her eyes. They see and feel her fear; the fear is palpable.

'Why are you so afraid, old witch? It is not for yourself, I think? No, it is for something or someone else.' Azi-Dhaka asks the question but looks for the answer, not in words but in a movement, a shift in the eyes or an intake of breath. Azi-Dhaka is the most skilled of Dragon Slayers for dragons are killed not so much by physical strength but by skill and art. His cunning is in finding his prey's weak spot.

As Azi-Dhaka speaks, he doesn't move his eyes from the kneeling Constance. 'The mother went into hiding but, deviously, she put the child in school in the city. From there, we have our only description of the child as being dark of hair and fair of face. A dragonlover too, which is why we have hunted so long and hard for him, but, from the age of eight, there has been no trace of him.'

'What has that to do with this girl we seek?' asks Samardashee, 'She, too, seems of an age with me and red of hair.'

At the words 'red hair' the murmur 'Mackenzie blood'

goes up. They ponder this amongst themselves.

'There is Mackenzie blood in more than a quarter of the population of the city, Your Highness,' Ochamore proclaims. 'All descended from one Scotsman.'

They laugh at the truth of this.

'And, like the Caledonian dragons, the colour passes on down through the generations – in the way the Caledonian green and purple is as distinctive in the dragons as the red is in the humans,' Ochamore, a veteran of more dragon fights than the rest of them put together, reliably informs them.

'Hair can be dyed,' says Azi-Dhaka, bringing the laughter to a halt. 'The boy was the colour of a Settler, making it easier for him to hide' – a fleeting thought crosses Azi-

Dhaka's mind – 'if that were his true colour.'

Once this deceit is voiced, the seed of doubt creeps into their minds – what other deceits might there be? Azi-Dhaka is the first to unearth it and raise the question.

'Are there really two of them?'

In the ensuing silence a picture, a flash of a red-haired girl, strikes King Samardashee's memory. He asks, 'Can Dragon Keepers breathe fire from their mouths?'

All eyes turn as one to look at the King.

'Aye, sire. The old tales talk of this.' This comes from the oldest warrior, the grey and grizzled Adib, known as The Wolf for his wisdom and strength. 'The father of this woman used to be at court: Jonas, Lord of the Flame, in times gone by.'

'You were a friend of this Jonas I seem to remember?'

Adib's horse shifts, restless. He reins it in. 'Yes, we were friends – back then.'

Ochamore moves towards Adib but King Samardashee intervenes, 'Pray, good Adib, tell us what you know of this Jonas. Where is he now?'

'I know not if he still lives, my King. Rumour was that he was living in the Rookeries.'

A shiver of tension passes amongst them as the Rookeries is the place where it is easy for anyone to disappear, whether they want to or not.

Adib continues, 'I know that he and this daughter here' – he gestures at Constance who listens, hardly daring to breathe – 'had a great falling out when the King, your father, married your mother. Lady Constance believed that she was betrothed to your father.'

'What do you say to this, witch?' King Samardashee demands.

'I was betrothed by the ring made from the greatest ruby ever found in this land. A gift from Chancellor Vlast to your father as a symbol of his brotherly love.'

As Constance speaks, the ruby shards in every warrior stir and they recognise that she speaks the truth. For the first time, they experience the bond that the ruby has created within them, the unity that, when all seven of them are together, gives the powers gifted to them a greater clarity so they transcend the ordinary and become magical. The King, with this new insight, sees the moment when his father places the ring on her hand and he has an inkling of the love in her and in his father – and, for the first time, he feels some compassion for this proud woman.

The loss of the ruby has exposed Constance. She has worn it for most of her life and it has protected her and strengthened her, keeping her safe from the hurt of her lost, cruel love. It has saved her from a possible life of martyrdom and self-loathing. She has grown so used to its powers that it is only now that she is without it that she feels her vulnerability. But she is intuitive enough to know that if the ring is no longer hers then she must have gained the strength and power with which it imbued her. The ring, the symbol of courtly love, has sustained her, and given her the love she was unable to give herself. Now she feels her heart beat with love for another once more. This gives her the strength to protect her young niece for Azra, this young innocent, has moved her too-long stony heart and brought her to life once more. For the first time in decades she moves beyond concern for herself. She watches and sees how the ruby affects the warriors.

The jovial-faced Ochamore is famed as the greatest warrior in the land. The shard enters the fighting hand of this wise old warrior. He looks down at it glowing beneath the skin and sees the others observing the ruby glow within each other. Young Merilin, out of the corner of her eye, sees the ruby light from the shard in her nose and looks fearful. Ochamore lays his hand on her shoulder to comfort her.

'Fear not. The ancients used to sew rubies under their skin to make them invincible. It is a great gift for a ruby to plant itself within us. Goodness knows it has protected Lady Constance here throughout the years!'

The flicker of fear turns to awe and respect as each warrior notes the ruby within themselves and each other.

In Ochamore, the hand that has slain so many in the name of king and country now pulses with the ruby shard. He has yet to learn what power this will give him but, for now, the hand on Merilin's shoulder transmits love and courage.

Adib has the shard in his heart and, for a brief yet immeasurable moment, he feels the love that once united King Qahir and Lady Constance.

Azi-Dhaka, the Dragon Slayer, feels it in his skin; the tingle of love shivers in excitement all over him, this hardened warrior, surprising and unnerving him in a way that battle never has.

Murray, the Sea-Warrior, feels the water rise in his body. Like a tidal wave, he feels the love and longing that the two once had.

However, the greatest surprise for them all is Baligh, the Stutterer. He drops to one knee by Constance and, after an interminable stalling on her name, 'L a d y Cccccccccccccccconsssssssss stttttancccccccccce,' he becomes what the stone has gifted him with, Baligh the Eloquent.

'You know the ruby would only leave you when the time was right. For you no longer need this symbol of courtly love for the truth is being revealed and, while this may seem to herald your darkest hour, soon your loyalty and faithfulness will be rewarded.'

All accept what Baligh is saying for, after the shard lodges in his tongue and he becomes Baligh the Eloquent, the real magic in the ruby's gift for Baligh becomes apparent in that he can taste the truth. So all present understand his words in their own way: the warriors hear his words as persuasiveness to help them; Constance hears them as being loyal and faithful to the love that has guided her all her life. The ruby once more saves Constance for each and every one of them feels more kindly and compassionate towards her as now they have some understanding of her.

So, the love with which the ring was given and received saves Constance but there is no joy for her in this as they now turn their attention where she wished, with all her heart, that they would not.

'We must waste no time. We must find this girl with the dragon for, with every hour, it gains size and strength,' the Dragon Slayer warns.

'So you must take us to them,' Ochamore demands of Constance.

But Samardashee knows that she will lead them astray as there is no gain for her in leading them to the girl and the dragon. He sees in her eyes what she will do so he turns to Merilin. 'What say you? Can you find them?'

'I say we go back to the camp and start from there, the last place we know they were.'

The King agrees and assigns Adib and Baligh to find Jonas in the city. Then he turns to Merilin and asks her advice. The shard in her nostril glows

as she turns her head towards
the forest.

'We return to the clearing
where the girl was last seen,'
she declares.

Constance despairs when
she hears this for she knows
how easily they tracked her
down. And, while her life has
been spared, she knows that
this is just the start – that they
will hunt Azra down to the end.

At the clearing, Merilin works
her way thoroughly over the
ground. She is the greatest
tracker in the land but now the
ruby shard has made her sense
of smell so acute that she can
scent a dragonfly's track across
the air and smell which plant a
butterfly has alighted on before
it headed her way – and now
she can smell the girl as

strongly as if she had just walked past.

She does not need to smell the ground. For her, the scent is on the wind. Her nostrils flare like a young stallion as she scents the air. 'She ate bacon and washed in rosewater so she is easy to follow.'

Constance pales as she realizes what this means. There is no hiding from a talented tracker like this.

'And what of the dragon?' demands the King.

She raises her nose to the wind then bends, to Constance's dismay, to around Azra's height where the backpack would be and nods. 'The dragon is with her.'

They mount their steeds and Constance is flung sideways across Azi-Dhaka's saddle. The painful, nauseating ride is some small penance for the guilt which she feels.

To their surprise, the trail leads towards the palace then veers away from the destroyed drawbridge and round the steep, sheer cliff that forms the impenetrable north face. They have to dismount and leave their horses to clamber down the sheer cliff.

King Samardashee begins to wonder if Merilin is right but she seems so assured as she checks the air at regular intervals. She sees his doubt and points to a single footprint in a patch of sand between two large rocks. A small footprint of a child or a woman – and it is fresh. The King nods, satisfied, and they continue.

The terrain becomes more difficult. For some time now they have been strung out in single file across the narrow ledge on the rock face when, all of a sudden, the trail runs out. Merilin looks puzzled; the King, confused.

'She cannot just disappear,' Merilin says.

They are all perplexed. Only Constance is momentarily relieved until Murray, the Sea-Warrior, steps forward. He examines the apparent sheer face of the cliff.

'To escape at sea you can always dive deeper.'

The others look at him with even greater confusion.

'Here, the only place to go deep is inside the mountain.' He taps all over what appears to be solid rock face until, at last, he finds what he is looking for, the pivot point. As he touches it the whole rock face in front of him opens up – a massive hidden door. It turns on less than a hand-span, revealing a fissure in the rocks. They squeeze through and find that the hand-hewn passage appears to continue deep beneath the palace cliffs.

King Samardashee gazes in astonishment. 'Who could make such a thing?' he asks in wonder as they all gaze in awe at the great cliff door.

'Dragon Keepers,' growls Azi-Dhaka. 'Of course, the Dragon's Nest was in the volcano under the palace; this must lead there. The passage is only large enough for a human and must have been built by human hand. The size of the door is trickery.'

'This must have taken aeons to carve,' remarks Samardashee. 'So it could not have been made during the Dragon Wars, there was not time or Keepers enough for this work.'

They follow each other on all fours, nose to rump, in the pitch dark, no sound but their laboured breathing as each one keeps up with the one ahead for none would want to lose hold of their fellow in the depths of such darkness.

Then, of a sudden, there is a faint light and the passage widens. They gaze up into the massive chamber and see the sunlight pouring in, miles above them. It is this glorious snatch of daylight that enables them to see how deep into the bowels of the earth they have crawled. There is an underground pool, the only means to move forward, so it is swim or turn back.

'I cannot swim,' says Samardashee.

So Ochamore steps forward, 'Sire, I would be honoured if I may teach you right now.' And, so saying, he hands his sword to Murray and indicates for the King to remove his.

The King hesitates but, having bounced this boy-king on his lap, Ochamore is bold enough to ignore royal protocol. He seizes the King and jumps with him into the icy water. The shocked King gasps for air as he feels Ochamore's strong arm around him.

'No! Unhand me!' gasps the King.

He's had enough of being treated like a boy. He throws Ochamore's arm off.

Ochamore sees he's over-reached himself. 'Kick your legs, sire. That's it, up and down. There is some urgency in this; if you don't you'll drown.'

Of necessity, the King learns to swim.

Murray makes Constance remove her skirts, binds the swords tight in them and urges her into the water before following with the precious swords. However, at the other side there are three passages off the underwater lake and, try as she might, Merilin can pick up no scent. The water has removed all traces of their prey.

Murray has kept abreast of Merilin this whole journey; the ruby shard in his heel has made him far fleeter of foot than any of them. Therefore, they agree that he and Merilin will examine the other two passages while the others continue into what they all agree looks like the main passage.

Constance has no idea which path young Azra has taken and her mind races, trying to think how she can warn her. Purposefully she slips, a stumbling kick that causes a small rock-fall that echoes through in the cavern but she has to be judicious. If they kill her she will be no help to Azra and she knows that, at the moment, for her the thread between life and death is a very fine line. Since the ring shattered she is feeling particularly vulnerable and the absence of it makes her realise that it has been her protection throughout the years. Now that is gone.

Azi-Dhaka gives Constance a warning look and she knows he is on to her so, for the next hundred yards, she keeps as silent as the others.

They hear a mewling cry echo in the air and they all pause, a pause that conveys that they know they have found them. They glance at each other and Azi-Dhaka speaks the word the warriors all dread, 'Dragon.'

They draw their swords and they see a dim light as the passage starts to widen. Constance picks her moment; she's calculating her next move because she knows that she will only get one chance as Azi-Dhaka has her under his watchful gaze. He will kill her the second she makes a move. She hesitates. Will her voice carry? How far away was the dragon? She watches the King sidestep a pile of scree, as does Azi-Dhaka. Constance stands on the unsafe stones and they shift and slide, taking her with them as she screams. Azi-Dhaka is on her in an instant, his blade at Constance's throat.

The King stays her hand. 'Gag her, but let her live.'

Azi-Dhaka can't resist a warning nick to Constance's neck with the knife as he gags her and whispers, 'I am not so lenient, old witch. One more false move from you and I will make sure I move faster than His Majesty.'

The scream forewarns me but I have nowhere to go. I have reached a dead end. I'm on a shelf overlooking a sheer drop into what looks like a bottomless chasm.

The sun shines through an opening high up in the roof of the cave – only to show that all is hopeless. A bridge spanning the chasm is broken off half-way across.

The dragon is too heavy for me to carry now. His growth is phenomenal. As we travelled through the forest, he fed constantly, ravenously devouring insects. By the time we reached the entrance to the cavern he was catching birds. The first one nearly choked him; I was terrified I was going to lose him. He regurgitated it then devoured the half digested remains. I was gagging watching him.

When we came to the pool in the cavern I had to put him down and he squealed with delight as he waddled and fell into the water, gulping and squealing. I dived in after him, fearful he was drowning, but his innate instinct kicked in and he began to swim.

It wasn't that I couldn't swim; Granpa had taught me to swim one summer. He told me, 'There are two ways you can die in the desert – from the heat or from drowning.' He took me to an underground pool in a cave in the wilderness. The walls were painted with pictures of dragons and humans in glorious colours, flying with them, swimming and playing. How he knew of this I don't know and, at the time, didn't think to ask him. But the sheer delight of swimming in the cool green water when outside was so unbearably hot was one of the moments of greatest pleasure in my life. Granpa said he would return with me each summer – but that was before Gramma found out and vetoed it, demanding he swear an oath he would never take me there again. She told me it was too dangerous and he was an old fool to have ever taken me there. At the time I thought she was afraid of me drowning – but now I think it may have been a place for training Dragon Keepers.

Now here we are, trapped on this ledge. We can't turn back but ahead is impossible. The only way out I can see is if he can fly across. There he will be safe, beyond their reach and by now, hopefully, he can fend for himself. If we're not together, I might be able to return to the forest.

Trapped on this ledge we don't stand a chance.

I have spent the morning trying to teach my new companion to fly. I'm sure he – if he is a 'he', I feel from his demeanour he is male – is big enough to fly across. He swam so instinctively, I am sure that flying, too, is innate in him. I've been encouraging him, demonstrating, spreading my cloak like wings and flapping – and it's as if he is smiling at me, bemused. I take the limited food supply and break it off in what I hope are tasty morsels and toss them out over the chasm for him to fetch but, so far, all he has done is elongate his neck and flick his tongue out, snapping up the insects as if to say, 'Is that the best you can do?'

I'm so frustrated – the gap is only about twenty feet wide. I'm sure it's an easy flight, even for a hatchling. Yet again I check *The Handbook,* but it reveals nothing. I get more impatient and he snaps at me. I snatch my fingers away.

'Stop being so stroppy!'

He does it again.

'All right, from now on I'm calling you Stroppy! Stroppy by nature so Stroppy by name,' I declare.

But soon I think that, maybe, I have made a mistake calling him Stroppy for he becomes more and more resistant. I look round for inspiration and notice droppings. I pick them up and they crumble to dust between my fingers – so it's not mice, it's what I'm hoping for.

I peer up into the shadowy corners of the chamber but can see nothing. I take a stone and throw it. My attempts at throwing food have helped improve my aim – the stone clatters into the shadows and there is a screech and a flurry of wings. The bats take flight and Stroppy flaps his wings and jumps, snapping one of them in his jaws, but his landing topples him over the edge. The ledge collapses, stones crumble under his clutching claws, tumbling into the abyss. I try to save him by his left leg but he is too heavy and I am pulled over the edge and dangle helplessly. My feet scrabble and I feel my toes kick at the rock edge, the stones falling all around me into the depths below. I hear a scream – and it is me. It's as if I'm hearing myself and the scream echoes, disturbing the bats, who panic past us.

Those seconds seem like an eternity – but we aren't

falling. Stroppy is hovering. Automatically his wings lift him and me with him. I look up and my heart lurches into my mouth as I see he is catching a bat. I dare not speak.

He glides back onto the ledge and I fall, trembling, to my knees, holding onto the ground for dear life. He barely notices me, his focus is on the food and, once more, his meal nearly chokes him. I throw my arms around his neck and hug him, grateful to be alive.

'Thank you! Thank you!'

'That's all right, child.'

The deep gruff voice startles me – where has it come from? Stroppy is eating the regurgitated bat.

'Stroppy, was that you?'

'I wish you wouldn't call me that.'

It *is* him! *The Handbook* was right; I can speak *Draco*. But how can he?

'How can you speak? Surely you have to learn?'

'I don't know. I just listened to you talking to the woman and yourself.'

'But that wasn't *Draco*.'

He shrugs his wings. 'I can understand you but not her.'

For a moment, this has distracted me from the peril we are in but one thing is sure, now that I am back in the comparative safety of the ledge, I won't persuade him to cross the abyss.

I really have no idea what to do. To go back is not an option but to move forward is impossible. I take check – we are safe here. I don't think they will find us. We have enough food for a day or two now that Stroppy has found his supply of bats.

I must find another name for him but nothing comes to mind.

As I sit I realise how a few days ago I knew little beyond my rooftop bed. Now here I am in this vast underground cavern with this dragon. He has been, unbeknown to me, closer to me than anyone in my life, in my nest of a bed.

The sun streams through the roof and a sunbeam spotlights *The Handbook* in my backpack. I pick it up and, at last, it is ready for me to read more. So I read aloud and Stroppy listens intently and I wonder idly if, somehow, my voice is familiar from the bedtime stories I told myself.

The Dragon Keeper's Handbook

Ancestory

The Dragons of Set are distinguished by their drab

yellow – grey colouring tinged with green. This enabled them to blend into the desert landscape when hunting. Since breeding with the Caledonian Dragons – with their colourful purple, green and blue scales – this useful hunting camouflage has been bred out of the Set Dragons. The Caledonian colours are now those associated with Dragons from Set.

Hatchling Dragons

A newly-hatched Dragon grows rapidly, especially in times of crisis.

In times of peace, the newborn Dragon can take anything from ten to fifty years to reach maturity. Dragon parents revel in helping their young enjoy these hatchling years for an extended time.

The times when this does happen go down in Dragon legend as halcyon days. Days of great renown. Tales are told of the tricks and fun these young yearlings get up to, the games they play for while they enjoy their immature years for longer they learn more tricks and have more fun. They grow into revered Dragons as, having had so much leisure and pleasure in their early years, they can impart much wisdom and give to the community a great sense of joy and well-being.

I glance at Stroppy – then at the p i c t u r e s o f D r a g o n development. He already looks about three years old. My heart sinks. Then I have a thought, maybe a new name will help?

A page turns, and there are the pictures of dragon flight.

'Why don't you show me this when I want it?' I ask the book.

It enlarges a picture of a Dragon Keeper sitting astride a young Dragon. A speech bubble rises from the Keeper's mouth. I try saying the word, 'Volanti'. Stroppy instantly spreads his wings.

It's at this moment we hear the scream.

'Aunt Constance,' I cry.

The scream is a warning and it blots all else from my mind. I have no time to think, fear or remember. Stroppy pricks up his ears and, without hesitating, I leap onto his back.

'Volanti!' I yell.

For a moment, I think he's going to obey. He spreads

his wings as if to take off but then he sniffs the air – and it stops him in his tracks. With a shrug and a roll, Stroppy flips me off his back. I'm trembling with relief at being back on the ground but this is instantly replaced by fear at what is coming towards us. A look that can only be described as a smile spreads across the dragon's face and that can only mean one thing – the Prince. I know there's no chance of getting him to fly now.

I hide in the shadows to one side of the passage, trembling, while Stroppy calls to his 'father'. The dragon is to one side, making him visible from the passage entrance. As the first warrior comes through, I trip him. He is so off-balance, bent almost double to ease through the low opening and the floor so uneven, that he falls straight into the chasm. I cry out in shock. I feel the blood drain from my face as his cry echoes, warning the others who now hold back. I am so stunned at what I've done that I don't regain my hiding place and see the Prince looking straight at me.

'I didn't mean to...I just meant to...' I stutter. Then I burst into tears.

It is just for a couple of seconds but it is enough for him to come up to me. I'm sure he would have killed me if I hadn't been such a pathetic heap. Now he, too, hesitates and a cry of greeting from a dragon that is now a head taller than him startles him. He raises his sword.

'No, no! He means you no harm, Prince; he thinks you are his father.'

'Kneel before your *King,* girl.' A massive warrior takes

me by the scruff of the neck and forces me to kneel.

I'm taken aback and ask Samardashee, 'You are *King?*'

'Aye, thanks to you to and your witchery. What do you mean – it thinks I'm its father?'

He and the dragon are eyeing each other, now, with a mutual respect tinged with wariness. The dragon and the King only have eyes for each other. Nothing else exists for them. The dragon gives a joyous whoop that echoes through the cavern and then he flies in loops of delight over the chasm. My mouth drops open in amazement, then, as he lands.

I am so mad at him I yell at him in anger and frustration, 'Thanks Stroppy! That's just typical!' My fear forgotten in my rage I turn on the King. 'I spend all morning trying to get him to fly and you come in and...'

'Stroppy?' The King turns with a raised eyebrow and a smile playing on his lips.

'I called him that – well I think it's a 'he' with the temper he has –   because he's just plain, well, *stroppy*. You know – bolshy, obstreperous.'

Stroppy lands on his back at the King's feet, wanting to have his stomach tickled. My heart is in my mouth. This is a dragon at its most vulnerable; his scales have not hardened and are still soft enough to penetrate easily and his belly, at this stage, is the softest spot of all – where it wants to be tickled and scratchcd by his father's 'claws'.

Not taking his eyes off the dragon for one second, King Samardashee asks, 'What is it doing?'

'I think it wants you to tickle its stomach,' I tell him.

Ochamore has seized my arms and is holding them behind my back. He has left Constance in the passage where she's lying down, motionless. I cannot tell if she's alive or not. I close my eyes. I cannot bear to watch as King Samardashee draws his sword as he steps towards Stroppy's exposed belly.

Then I hear Stroppy laughing, a strange hiccupping dragon laugh and, when I open my eyes, there is King Samardashee tickling him with his sword. Slowly, a smile spreads over King Samardashee's face too. I can't believe it – and neither can Ochamore.

Ochamore speaks in a low voice, 'Sire, this is the one time when a dragon is vulnerable…and the belly is the softest spot. It may seem...' he struggles for the right word, '… quite sweet right now but this is a dangerous creature.'

'Exactly! And it believes I'm its father and is bonded to me for life. I think this gives us a great opportunity. Don't you?'

Then something incredible happens. Stroppy is over onto his feet, his wings fully extended as he roars savagely. But it is not any of us that his anger is directed towards – it's at two men walking in mid-air across the abyss.

The men have stepped off the broken bridge and are coming towards us, one behind the other, through empty space. Suspended in mid-air, the one in front scatters a thin layer of sand that they step onto. The ribbon of sand stays, revealing the once invisible footpath. The King stares, disbelieving too as they traverse the gap and reach us. The more regal of the two laughs disdainfully at our astonishment.

'How on earth did you do that, Uncle Vlast?' asks the King.

'Ah, Samardashee, you should never believe your eyes. This world is all an illusion and if you only rely upon one sense you will remain, as this young woman has, trapped.' He gestures towards me. 'You had no courage, child, no faith or trust. The way out was before you but you were too fearful to see it.'

There is something about this man that makes the hair on the back of my neck stand on end. How does he know I have been trapped here? I feel the blood drain from my face again as I realise he must have been watching us. Does he know who I am? And how did he cross the chasm on a few grains of sand?

'What sorcery is this, Chancellor Vlast?' Ochamore demands.

'Oh, Ochamore! If we relied on you warriors, the kingdom would be in a sorry state.'

Ochamore goes to examine the bridge and he, too, steps onto what looks like sand suspended mid-air. He kicks the sand aside – but he still stands mid-air.

Vlast surveys them. 'A select little band we have here. So, sire, I suggest you rid the world of these meddlesome creatures,' he indicates towards Stroppy and me, 'and then we can get down to business.'

Vlast's henchman stands mute and massive; he towers over Ochamore and stands between him and Vlast so the King and I are on the narrowest

316

section of ledge and the dragon behind us.

King Samardashee comes towards me with his sword and I screech, 'Oh my giddy fiddy!'

He halts, looks at me with one eyebrow raised and, to our surprise, we both start to laugh hysterically – and the dragon joins in. We're a trio collapsed in laughter.

When he catches his breath he asks, 'What on *earth* was that?'

'What?'

'Oh my giddy *what?*'

'Oh my giddy fiddy'I say, slightly embarrassed now, as I wipe tears from my eyes.

The sixteen years of despising and loathing this boy from what I learnt in school just dissipates in this bout of spontaneous laughter. The tension, the fear, they all dissolve in this unstoppable laughter.

Stroppy gives us a quizzical look as if to say, 'I don't know what they're laughing at but I'm having some of that,' and his wings shudder and flap as he gives his dragon laugh.

But Vlast isn't laughing. He draws his sword and comes towards me. I step back.

Do you ever have that moment when you know you shouldn't have done something? This was one of those. I step back into nothing and my weight is on that foot so there is no going back. I topple backwards into the chasm. I fall so fast I can hear my scream way up above me. I am terrified, powerless. Then, something instinctive kicks in. I seize two fistfuls of the Prince's cape that I am still wearing – and the thought that only last night he was a prince, now he is King, flashes into my mind and that random thought knocks aside the terror of falling. I clutch the cape and I spread my arms – wide – just as I'd done teaching the dragon to fly. I turn and the air fills the cape and slows me down. My fall is transformed into a glide and my fear turns to hope. I still can't see the bottom – but now I can hear something and it sounds like water. I turn upright and enter the water feet first. One minute I'm gliding through the air with my amazing cape and the next the cape that has just saved me is weighing me down, drowning me in the water.

Love and friendship in the midst of death and destruction

Vlast watches with satisfaction as the girl falls then turns to Samardashee.

'I have waited for this moment a very long time. If I was one to believe in destiny, I would say you had someone watching over you for each time I have come close to ending your pathetic little life, something has always intervened. But no more – for now it is *my* moment. You have been mollycoddled and surrounded by those sycophants who worshipped the very ground you walked on.'

Immediately, Ochamore gives a roar as he draws his sword but Vlast's henchman has the advantage of him, being twice Ochamore's size, and seizes him in his massive arms, crushing the breath out of him.

Meanwhile, Vlast disarms the astounded King and takes out his dagger, his favourite weapon, and closes in for the kill – but he has not reckoned on Stroppy. In Vlast's experience, dragons despise humans and are only too happy to eat them for breakfast. This young dragon he sees as no real threat. He has killed far worse, usually by stealth, feeding them poisoned carcasses then delivering the final blow with his dagger through their eyes. He has taken great pleasure in the fact that, for most dragons, the last thing they see on this earth is him.

So, as Vlast steps in for the kill, Stroppy thrusts his head between the King's legs and opens his mouth, issuing forth a blast of dragon fire. The only thing that saves Vlast is that this is Stroppy's first breath of dragon fire. If Stroppy had been any older or more practised in his fire-breathing then Vlast would have been totally fried. As it is, the young dragon's main aim is protecting Samardashee and the fire is more of a warning, but a warning blast of fire from a dragon's mouth is enough to shrivel and waste Vlast's right arm. It is incinerated, burnt away to a shrivelled stump at his shoulder.

Now Samardashee is astride the dragon and Stroppy takes off in flight, swooping down into the bowels of the earth –

way,

        way,

                w a

        y

                d o

                w n

322

bel
o w

.

As they fly, Samardashee talks to Stroppy, 'Did you see that? I knew there was something about him. He has always tried to manipulate me and I've never trusted him but my father was always telling me to respect him. How can you respect someone you think has *always* been out to get you? Look, Stroppy, I think we should find a better name for you but, if you don't mind, I'll call you that for now. Okay?

The dragon gives a snort that Samardashee takes for a 'Yes' but then his flight becomes erratic. He bumps into the cliff face and they crash-land in a tangled, bruised heap at the bottom of the chasm. Stroppy lies there, eyes closed, and Samardashee examines him, asking, 'What's wrong?'

323

There's a terrible grumbling sound coming from the region of Stroppy's stomach.

'Food? Do you need food?'

He realises that the dragon needs to eat, but what? And how, in this barren place, is he going to find anything that will satisfy a dragon? He walks towards the water and watches the pool. Something is swimming there – lots of them. They don't look like fish as he knows them but they do look like possible food.

As he's puzzling how to get the fish, a voice booms in his memory from a time he spent with Murray, the Sea-warrior, 'When I was a lad in Scotland we used to tickle the fish with our bare hands. You just put your hand in the water, keep it *very* still until you've tricked it into trusting you, and then gently, gently you ease your finger along its belly up to its gills and *whoosh* – dinner!' With the uproarious laugh ringing in his mind, Samardashee has a go. At first he is reluctant to put his hand in among these strange fish but a glance at Stroppy makes him realise he has to act quickly. The strange feel of the fish startles him and both fish and Samardashee start back in surprise. He tries a second time but the fish wriggles away immediately. A third, a fourth – he goes until he loses count. It doesn't get any easier. He sits back in despair. He doesn't think this will ever work. Then he spies a tail under a rock. Carefully he approaches it, easing his finger gently along the relaxed body of the fish. It allows him to tickle and, holding his breath, he gives a final flick and he has it! At last he feels the *whoosh* in Murray's story.

The thrill of his first catch exhilarates him. Proudly, he takes it to the dragon, the exhausted Stroppy who looks at him with one curious eye. He feeds the fish to him and Stroppy downs it in one gulp.

'Hmm, I think I'm going to need a lot more than that.'

After he has fed Stroppy a dozen or so fish, the dragon regains his strength and is able to get up and comes to the water's edge. Then, he dives in, his wings folded into his side; he swims eel-like through the water, mouth open, swallowing fish until he's satisfied.

He emerges from the water and deposits a mouthful of fish at Samardashee's feet, belches and, as he does, flames shoot out of his nostrils and fry the fish. Samardashee hesitates for a brief second then his belly growls, telling him not to be so stupid. He picks up a fish and starts to nibble at it. To his surprise, it's not just good – it's fantastic! He wolfs it down and soon he's as bloated as Stroppy.

It's only now, lying on his back, staring up at the vast walls of the chamber, that Samardashee has time to review the situation – and it's not good. He still has difficulty thinking of himself as King, especially in his current situation. He may have bonded to this creature but it is a fearsome beast and, seeing how it literally disarmed Vlast, he does not want to take any chances with it.

Even if he can persuade Stroppy to fly back up, he can't go back to the palace. Now that Vlast has revealed his true colours he will have taken over the palace with some story to discredit Samardashee. That,

Samardashee thinks to himself, would be quite easy – I've burnt down the Forest of Discontent and disappeared with a dragon after it blasted my uncle's arm off. It is unlikely Ochamore is still alive, the only one who can verify his story – or would he, too, think that he's in league with the dragon? He looks at this creature that, for all his life he has been brought up to fear and hate, and he feels neither of those things.

'Ah, Stroppy, what do I do?' He picks up the jewel-encrusted crown that he'd placed for safekeeping on a rock when he was fishing. He examines it closely for the first time, turning it in his fingers.

'Well, I suppose this means that I'm still King.'

He stops, still holding the crown. He holds it carefully, the crown is framing what he can see. The stones on the beach are chipped where he has kicked at them – and he sees the glint in the light like the jewels in his crown. They are jewels!

'Why am I such a dunderhead? Of course Vlast was surprised to see me! He wasn't expecting to see me at all. He hadn't come down here for me – but for these.' He picks up an emerald and shows it to a disinterested Stroppy.

It's as if all the small details of Samardashee's life suddenly fall into place: the way his uncle was always on mysterious business, the ruby ring, if Constance is to be believed, was given to her by Chancellor Vlast. It was his uncle who oversaw the royal jewels. Samardashee had never thought to ask where they had come from but, if the stories of the Dragon's Nest being made of precious stones were true, then no wonder Vlast had been so eager to get rid of all the dragons.

'We aren't safe, Stroppy, neither of us. We need to get out of here or we are doomed,' Samardashee tells him as he starts to look for a way out.

The river seems the obvious way out. There is a shore in the distance; it doesn't look any further than Samardashee's first swim so he shows Stroppy where he's heading and they set off together.

But it is much more difficult than his previous swim. He has underestimated the distance and, gasping and spluttering after swimming less than half way as he chokes on another mouthful of water, Samardashee knows he can't swim much further. But Stroppy comes to the rescue. He has dived and comes up under Samardashee who clings, gasping, onto the spine on the dragon's head. Samardashee hauls himself up and looks around. From this vantage point he can see around the bend in the river – and here, at last, he thinks his luck has changed.

He persuades Stroppy to swim over to the cove that has caught his attention. In a natural inlet lies a long, flat-bottomed boat. Samardashee climbs into it. A pole lies in it. Samardashee has only ever been in the boat on the castle moat. This is different. He has used oars but not a pole. He has seen it in pictures and places his pole in the water to push off – but his first attempt lands him in the water. Then he uses his hands but soon gets tired of so much effort for so little gain. So, he tries the pole again and, this time, he gets more movement and starts guiding the boat through the tunnel, calling out, 'Look! Now I've got it. Look at me!' It takes him some time to realise that it's Stroppy pushing the boat. In the end, he sits down and lets the dragon push him through the underground passageways.

He gazes in awe at his surroundings. For as the little boat goes deeper into the volcano, the walls begin to reflect the light – green, ruby and gold – more beautiful than the handcrafted tiled baths in the palace. Parts seem transparent, that the light comes from within them, and it dawns on him that these are jewels.

His awe turns to fear as he sees another natural cove with a small pebble-covered beach and there's a body lying there! It's Azra! His heart skips a beat. Is she dead? Without thinking, he jumps out the boat to go to her. His concern surprises him. He had wanted to kill her but now that she might be dead he realises that he doesn't want that at all. No, he doesn't want that at all – quite the opposite.

Samardashee gazes down on her still form, not daring to touch her. Stroppy lopes over and nudges her. She coughs, splutters and throws up the water she has swallowed.

'How did you get here?' the King asks gently.

'The... river...brought... me.'

She is shivering. He takes off the wet cloak and persuades Stroppy to breathe fire – which he does, for Samardashee. One dragon breath is enough to dry their sodden clothes.

'Why are you helping me?' Azra asks.

'Because you need it – and I think we stand more

chance of getting out of here together than alone.'

Azra watches him closely. She feels closer to this young king than anyone she has known – not that she has had much contact with anyone but her school days have coloured her view of those her own age. This Samardashee, she hopes and wishes, will become a friend.

Samardashee is looking at the river. 'There's no current. How could the river bring you?'

'I nearly drowned it was so strong.' She gazes in amazement at the still water. Azra is puzzled and annoyed as she regains her strength. 'It was intense...'

Laughing, Samardashee wades into the water but his laughter stops abruptly as a sudden massive wave surges and he is swept off his feet as the river becomes a fast-moving torrent. At first, Azra laughs at the shock and surprise on his face but it dies on her lips as she sees the danger he is in. She grabs the pole from the punt and holds it out for him and, after some struggle with a distressed Stroppy pushing Samardashee from behind, manages to hauls him to safety. The King is safe but a second wave takes Stroppy unawares and sweeps him and the boat downstream.

The pair watch, helpless.

'What can we do?' Azra asks.

Samardashee looks at the river; now that the second wave has passed, its churning waters are settling. Shaken, he sits recovering on the shore and begins to wonder, 'How can that be? That one moment it is so calm I have to work hard to move through it, the next it's so strong it almost sweeps me away?'

Azra shrugs, 'I don't know much about water.'

'Me neither. Maybe it's like the desert when sandstorms sweep through? But where is the wind?' Samardashee looks around at the vast river and up into the 'sky' of the cave. 'I have read of such things as this but dismissed them as fiction, mere stories.' He looks at the pole in her hand. 'And who made this?'

But Azra is looking beyond him, her eyes widen in wonder and, at first, disbelief. 'I think they are the answer.'

He turns to see two white-haired people standing, watching them.
They are so white they are almost translucent.

Somewhere in the depths of my memory, I recall Granpa Jonas telling me a story about the White People. They were so white they could not bear the sun and people both feared them, believing them to be cursed, yet also believing them to be magical. People hunted them to steal the magic that they believed was in their bodies. But Granpa told me neither was true. 'They are human, just like you and me,' he told me. But now I set eyes on them I am not so sure.

I cannot tell if they are male or female, both have long wavy hair and a delicacy of features. The tall one speaks first, in a tongue that I don't understand – but it is obviously a command and, that instant, a net drops on us from above.

Samardashee is furious and struggles to try to free himself but as soon as it touches me I know it is no use – this is no ordinary net, this is a giant spider's web and the more he struggles the more the sticky strands ensnare him. One of them reaches out and I feel a cool hand, or assume that is what it is, touch me on the neck and I remember no more.

I wake and we are now surrounded by the White Folk. Still bound in the web, I see that Samardashee is wrapped tightly, parcelled in the silken thread. He, too, seems to be out cold but as soon as he comes round he protests, 'Release me at once! I am your King, Samardashee.'

They laugh. 'You, boy, are no king. We know King Qahir, the so-called ruler of Set.'

'He is – was my father. Now he is dead and I am King of Set.'

They speak excitedly to each other then one turns to Samardashee and says, 'If the King is dead then King Vlast must rule the land.'

At this, Samardashee stops struggling. 'Vlast? Why would you think my uncle would be King?'

'Because that is what he promised us, that when the King dies he will become King and we will regain our rightful place in the forest – free from fear and attack.'

This exchange is translated and the news sets up a great buzz of excitement that passes among the White Folk like wildfire. Some start whooping and dancing.

I don't know about Samardashee but hearing that makes my skin crawl. I feel as if tiny ants are racing all over my skin. Throughout this, I wonder where Stroppy might be but there is no sign of him – he's disappeared.

Samardashee has gone very quiet at the mention of Vlast and I quiz him as they lead us through the dimly-lit tunnel.

'Why are you so quiet?'

'Because I think I see the bigger picture and that Vlast is behind all this.' He indicates the vast underground city they have led us to. The buildings aren't just decorated with gemstones; the walls are made of them. They give off a constant flicker of colour in the cave's soft light. There are trees and hanging gardens growing in tiny pockets on the rock face. All around are tables set out with families and friends eating and chatting. They invite us to sit down to a meal of fish and some sort of greens but Samardashee says he isn't hungry. It is all very friendly and sociable and, once they have us as prisoners, they are very hospitable – but Samardashee will have none of it.

There is a pulsing, booming noise that vibrates right through the rock all around us. The people start dancing. Drums are brought out and those that aren't dancing are drumming. I put my hands over my ears, which makes the White Folk laugh. I try to see where the sound is coming from. Our guide points to one of their number who is blowing into a hole in the rock, a fault-line that forms a channel for the sound, a natural didgeridoo.

Suddenly, the didge sound changes and becomes like an alarm call and every man, woman and child in the place gets up and files out of the vast chamber. We follow them into this vast, circular shaft. They pick up their tools – small hammers and tiny picks. Some of them are hoisted up in baskets and tied into place so they hang, suspended mid-air like insects, as they chip away at the shaft walls.

' D i a m o n d s , ' Samardashee tells me, 'rubies and emeralds. This is why Vlast wanted the dragons killed; he knew it was the only way to get to their lair...'

'...to mine the precious stones,' I finish his sentence for him. We are talking quietly, both aware that although the White Folk have removed the net, we are surrounded by them. They are all keeping a few paces away from us but it feels like we are being escorted rather than walking of our own free will.

All the years of hiding, of death and destruction, rise up in me.

'The Dragon Wars were all for this?' I kick at a basket of gems and one large red stone rolls to my feet. I pick it up. 'What's this?'

'These look like the stones that Vlast is building the new Great Hall for the palace with.' Samardashee says as I hand it to him but the stone is seized from our grasp.

'Not to touch,' says the implacable escort, carefully replacing the stone in the basket, which is swiftly removed by one of the others.

'Why is he building a new hall? How long has it been going on?' I ask.

'He started building it when I was born, after the Naming. He said we needed to build a new hall untainted by the curse.'

'Sixteen years!' I exclaim.

Samardashee shrugs in resignation. 'I remember every time my father questioned him about it there was some long tale; he needed this special stone, needed to build something extra. It was said it would be ready this year, for my coming of age.'

'And is it?'

'I don't know. The celebrations were kept secret from me – I only rehearsed the protocols, everything else was a mystery to be unveiled on the day. But the hall and its attendant buildings now dwarf the palace. Vlast claims he is using the original plans that my great-great grandfather never finished. The palace as we know it, according to Vlast, was only meant to be a retreat, an inner sanctum in times of emergency.'

I'm smiling to myself as he speaks.

'What are you smiling at?'

'You talk like a history book.'

He looks shocked and then gives a stiff bow and apologises then explains how he was always taught alone, the only friend his own age was the stable boy – all they talked about was horses. He thanks me for being so honest as all his life he has been surrounded by people saying what they thought he wanted to hear. He calls my honesty 'refreshing'.

I must sound as strange to him. Until I was eight I could hear only too clearly what people were saying about me.

The baskets lined up must be the result of the morning's efforts – and they are full of the red stones.

'What are these?' Samardashee asks.

The young boy in front of us blurts out, 'Jasper,' as the man escorting us is saying, 'That is none of your business.' The boy looks up and apologises to the man who tells the boy, 'Remember: The less they know the better.'

The boy responds with, 'The less they know the less they have to forget.'

'Why do you say that?' I demand.

He shrugs and replies, 'It is one of our teachings with regard to those who find their way here. But for you it is of no matter.'

For a moment I think we are special, that they don't mind us knowing because Samardashee is King. Then the boy shoves me and something in the way he does it and the way he commands us, 'Move,' makes me feel very afraid.

'I think they're going to kill us,' I whisper to Samardashee.

'They wouldn't dare!' Then he stops and realises that I may be right. 'If Vlast told them when he became King he would give them their freedom...'

'Then they'll want you out of the way.'

Suddenly, it all begins to make sense. 'Vlast didn't know we would come to the caves – he was coming here! It was just chance, coincidence that he found us.

Samardashee sees it too. 'The invisible bridge is how he kept all this secret. Only he and his mute henchman must know of it.'

'But how does he explain where he gets all the stones from?' I want to know.

'Because of the feud between the palace and the city – he would always take charge of the 'delicate' negotiations.' King Samardashee gets more and more excited as things fall into place for him. 'I've heard the wagons in the night! The stones are delivered at night!'

'And if they know him and they are supplying the stones there must be a way down.'

In my excitement I've almost forgotten that we are surrounded by White Folk. The path forks and most White Folk take the path to the right. The Folk who go to the right look like a work party, wearing belts with tools and carrying what must be food in their small containers. Only two remain with us – a man and a woman. She hasn't spoken a word but her hand gripping my arm makes it clear, as does the staff he carries which I now see is a weapon – we are prisoners.

I know it's a stupid question, that Samardashee has no more idea of the answer than I, and that our guard will not answer, yet still I ask it, 'Where are they taking us now?'

How To Charm A Prince

We have the answer sooner than either of us would like.

They seize us and tie us to the ground, spread-eagled, clamping our arms and legs in what seem to be metal manacles, but a metal I have never seen before. It moulds to my wrists, close-fitting as cloth or rope, but it becomes rigid as soon as it is fixed onto me and sings like steel when it hits the rock.

Then, slowly, the sky seems to be coming towards us.

I am terrified! For a moment I can't figure out what is happening. Then I realise that the ground is vibrating beneath me – it isn't the sky moving, it is the earth.

'What's happening?' I scream.

'I think we're on some kind of platform.'

He is right; we are rising up through the volcanic shaft.

The shaft narrows towards the top so the platform fits tight and the 'plug' that we are strapped to serves the dual purpose of shading the workers as well as exposing us to the blistering heat of the overhead sun. From the position of the sun, I can tell it is early morning – we have been underground all night!

Samardashee looks despondent. 'No-one will think of looking for us here,' he says.

'Who can you trust? Who is loyal to you?'

'The six warriors who came with me but who knows how many are still alive. At court – I have no idea. Most follow the Crown but, if Vlast has persuaded them that he is the rightful King...'

'And you have flown off with a dragon...'

'Wherever he may be...There are so few of them left at court, the White Folk could easily overwhelm them.' Samardashee is struggling to get free; his only thought is to escape. 'We've got a couple of hours before the high sun. Come on, why don't you try?'

'I want to find out more about you.'

'Here, like this?'

'Well, it's better than having you or your uncle try to kill me.'

'Are you kidding? *This* is how they are killing us.'

'Oh! I'm not going to die like this.'

'Okay, Miss Azra, how are you going to die?'

'I don't mean that I can *see* how I'm going to die. That's my aunt's thing, prophecy I mean.'

That was definitely the wrong thing to say. He is furious when I mention my aunt so I decide to stop wasting time and distract him. I fold my thumbs in on themselves and slide my hands out of the iron rings that bind me to the platform. Samardashee looks at me in astonishment.

'I'm double-jointed,' I tell him, demonstrating how I can fold my hands back on themselves. 'It's the one thing that stopped the other kids picking on me – it freaked them out so much.'

'So why didn't you do that sooner?'

'I thought you'd feel bad if I got free so quickly because I'm free and you're not.'

He looks at his shackles and realises that I'm right; this hasn't helped him at all. I stand up and look out over the horizon. To the south and west the rocky slopes of the volcano stretch out for miles. In the distance are the Dryseas.

'It's no use you looking out that way; our only hope is to get help from the palace.'

'*Our* only hope? You mean *yours*! I'm as good as dead if I go to the palace. And, actually, I don't think you have much hope there either from the sound of it.'

'You're not going to leave me!'

'If I see anyone I'll send them to help you,' I tell him and he looks at me, horrified. 'That was a joke,' I add quickly.

'Then I don't think much of your sense of humour.' He looks sullen so my attempt to lighten a dire situation has only made it worse.

The sun is now, by my reckoning, at around eleven-thirty, so to get any help at all before the scorching midday sun does its damage is nigh on impossible. I need time to think, to be alone. I take off my cloak and I feel the *clunk* of a large pebble, the shape *The Handbook* has been hiding as, presumably, since it hit the water. I fold the cloak and sit on it. Slowly, as my fingers touch it, *The Handbook* changes into book form and opens up for me.

As I start to read I'm interrupted by Samardashee yelling at me, 'You're *reading*! I'm here pinned out like a piece of meat to dry in the sun and all you can think of doing is *read*!'

'Just shut up – please.'

I think the *please* did it; he wasn't expecting that. What I read excites me. I read it out loud to him.

"A Dragon may respond to an appeal for help by using

the Call of the Dragon. This is produced, in humans, from the back of the throat and calling, *Kreekreekreekaakree...*'

I stand up and clear my throat, throw back my head and call out as loud as I can, '*Kreekreekreekaakree...*'

Even to my ears it sounds pathetic.

'What on earth are you doing?' Samardashee asks.

'*The Call of The Dragon.*'

'Well I wouldn't come if you called me like that.'

'You're not a dragon,' I retort, hurt that he is so negative towards me.

'Wait. Don't get upset. I meant that it just doesn't sound right.'

'And how would you know?'

He shrugs. Well, sort of, as best he can with his hands manacled. 'I've got a good ear. You went…' and he repeats it note for note, exactly how I'd done *The Call*. 'It will carry further if you do this…' and he makes *The Call*. I don't know how he did it but somehow it was the same – but totally different.

'Kreekreekreeka akree…'

The sound travels, across to the palace on the horizon, echoing off its walls. It races across the desert. It vibrates in the forest and, most of all, it rumbles, somehow, beneath our feet through the shaft below us.

I stand, mouth open in amazement. 'How did you do that?'

'I like to sing and, as I said, I've a good ear.'

'But that is astonish…' I never finish for the sun darkens and there is a tremendous booming noise. I look up and it's the beat of massive wings and there, in front of us, is – a DRAGON. But what a dragon! It is magnificent – massive green wings with green, blue and purple iridescent scales, a white and yellow underbelly, huge flaring nostrils and green and black eyes flecked with gold. I am too awestruck to be afraid – and if I'd been afraid there was nothing I could have done to escape from this magnificent creature anyway.

The question uppermost in my mind is, 'Where have you come from?' I get the answer. It lifts its head and gives a roar that sounds like it's furious.

'Can you help us, Dragon?' I ask in *Draco*.

In answer it gives another roar of rage.

'What did you say?' demands Samardashee.

The dragon raises one massive claw and slashes at Samardashee. Samardashee and I scream simultaneously. I can't bear to look and it all goes quiet.

I wait, expecting the worst, and there's nothing. Slowly – very, very slowly, I open my eyes.

The dragon has its claw raised and takes another swipe at Samardashee. I scramble up its hind leg onto its back. What I hope to do there, I've no idea but you try coming up with something better when you're facing a dragon three times your size.

The dragon turns its head and looks at me disdainfully, holds up the shackle that it has torn out with its claw and tosses it aside.

Samardashee sits up, rubbing his wrists, and looks at the dragon. 'I wondered where you'd got to.'

'Stroppy?' I ask.

'Of course it's Stroppy,' Samardashee says.

The dragon snorts, 'Not much of a Dragon Keeper if you can't even recognise me.'

No matter how awe-inspiring and terrifying his exterior, the tone of voice could only be him.

'Stroppy!' I cry and hug him round the neck.

He gives a haughty toss to his head. 'It's not much of a name for a dragon,' he says haughtily.

'You're talking to him! How?' Samardashee says in astonishment.

I shrug. 'It's something Dragon Keepers are born with,

apparently. I can speak *Draco,* the silver tongue of dragons,' I hesitate as I say this for I remember how this was a term of abuse at school for anyone who spoke differently.

To my surprise, all Samardashee says is, 'Well translate for me then!'

'Okay.' So I translate what Stroppy has said so far then turn to continue the conversation with Stroppy, 'You're right. We need to decide on your name but you must admit you do tend to be a bit...'

'Be careful,' the dragon warns with a wisdom that hits home. 'When you label something then that is what you get.'

When I translate, Samardashee is undeterred, 'Stroppy by name, stroppy by nature I say.'

'Although I think he's got a point,' I tell Samardashee.

I ponder out loud, 'You appear from your colouring to be descended from the Caledonian dragons so I think we should give you a Scottish name.'

Samardashee is more serious now and after some moments he says, 'My first tutor was called Kenneth, a really fiery man. He told me it derives from the Scots name of *Cinaed* meaning *born of fire.* Which I think fits you well.'

The moment he says this I have tingles down my spine and the dragon lifts his head and snorts with pride.

'*Cinaed,*' says the dragon and nods, 'It's perfect.'

'From now on, I am going to call you your given name, *Cinaed.* In fact I think it should be *Cinaed the Magnificent.* You've

transformed overnight!'
Samardashee announces.

'I have, haven't I?' And
somehow it doesn't sound
pompous, just matter of fact
when he says it.

It's now that I see how
much Samardashee has
changed. This dragon has won
him over, charmed him. There
is a mutual respect between the
two.

'Is that usual, that
dragons grow and change so
fast?' asks Samardashee.

Cinaed looks as
mysterious as he can, as if he
isn't giving anything away, but
I think he doesn't know either.
He shrugs his wings and that is
enough to turn the page of *The
Dragon Keeper's Handbook* to
the chapter *Dragon Puberty
and Adolescence.*

I read it out aloud,

'A Dragon's development can be greatly accelerated according to the experiences and circumstances surrounding it. For example, a Dragon born into dangerous times can have its growth accelerated from years to a matter of hours or, in cases of extreme adversity, mere minutes. Also, a Dragon forced from necessity to mature and behave in the manner of an adult Dragon has been known to develop its iridescent scales – normally only found in mature adult dragons – overnight.'

As I say this we both turn to look at Cinaed's iridescent wings, which he adjusts with a shrug that he tries to make nonchalant, to show them off even more.

'When it has to assume the nature and role of an adult Dragon, then it becomes one almost instantly.

In Dragon development, it is the nature of the Dragon's life journey that matures it rather than the number of years. Some Dragons may remain in their immature state for hundreds of years if they never encounter the challenges that allow them to mature. Similarly, Dragons that encounter challenges but are unable to rise and face them will not develop until they meet a challenge that they do face.'

As I stop reading, Samardashee and I look at Cinaed in wonder.

'So what happened to you?' we chorus.

I translate Cinaed's reply just as I have translated *The Handbook* for Cinaed.

'I wish you could both understand each other,' I wail. 'It's hard work translating.'

'I am beginning to understand your tongue,' Cinaed announces, 'but I do not wish to speak it.'

'And you' – Samardashee turns to me – 'will teach me *Draco* as soon as we get out of this mess,' he commands.

He is really so bossy. I know he's used to being obeyed but really this king thing is a bit much...

My reply dies on my lips because Cinaed has started his tale...

Transforming A Monster
Into A Myth

Cinaed's Tale

'We have not much time, I have to go back, but it is important that you know this. When I saw the White Folk, something in me knew they are even more antagonistic towards dragons than the Settlers. I could feel they have even more fear of us because they are living in our Kingdom. They have made their settlement in the Dragons' Lair.'

I translate this and immediately Samardashee asks,
'How do you know all this?'
I translate this reluctantly and Cinaed looks at him as if this remark is beneath contempt. I give Samardashee a

look to tell him to shut up and listen; it's hard enough translating without him interrupting.

'When you know, you know. And what came to pass confirmed the knowing.'

He takes a deep breath, his nostrils flaring, 'To look at the White Folk quenched the fire in me – and I found out why. When they took you I followed and it made my heart cold to see the destruction they have wreaked down there. They have destroyed the Dragons' Nests, taken the stones and built their pathetic city with them. The sight made me foolish and weak. I just stood and gazed. I felt my strength leave me. Because my heart was cold, the fire in me was out so they were able to take me prisoner, ensnaring me in their spider web nets.'

He scratches at the rock with his talon, carving his distress into the stone.
'I was ashamed for I had fire when I burnt your enemy and when I cooked food for you.'

I can feel his shame at his helplessness. But, as he talks, I feel the hope rise up in him.

'Then, thinking of you made my heart warm and I could feel the fire stir in me. So I tried and could breathe this small fire out, it could not burn the web net but it warmed the walls of my prison – and then...' He pauses, savouring the memory of that moment, '...I could see in the walls the eggs of my kin.'

I lean forward eagerly when I hear this. I hear Samardashee cry out but I don't look at him, a decision I was to regret. If I had turned I might have seen his reaction and been able to prevent what happened later but at the time all I could think of, and say, was, 'Dragon's eggs!'

Cinaed pauses and his dragon eyes cloud over at the pain of that vivid memory. '...my brothers and sisters within their shells, imprisoned in the walls.'

My blood runs cold at this. His emotion is so strong I can *feel* how it must have been for him, to see all his kind trapped in the walls of the White Folk.

'I don't understand,' says Samardashee.

'When a dragon – or Dragon Keeper – breathes fire onto a dragon's egg you can see the baby dragon inside. In fact, it's the only way to tell the difference between a stone and an egg. This is how they protect the unborn dragon.'

'So why did your mother take an egg into the city?'

I remember my first sight of Cinaed inside his egg when I first breathed fire onto it, how vulnerable he looked and I sense how protective my mother must have felt.

'She took it to keep it safe, she would be afraid that whoever destroyed the Dragon's Nest would also destroy the dragons' eggs.'

We both sit silent at the vision Cinaed's story has brought up.

'This made the fire burn strong in me and I began to hatch out my brothers and sisters,' Cinaed tells us with more than a hint of pride at being able to free them.

'You did what?'
Samardashee's voice is cold.

Cinaed doesn't appear to pick up on it but I do and I sense something has changed for Samardashee. I watch him closely and see that, for him, a single 'tame' dragon that has bonded to him is a very different thing to a whole nest of dragons. He looks threatened but I dismiss it in my eagerness to know more.

'How did you do it? You were tied up in the web net!'

'I could still breathe.' All pride has left his voice, he sounds so modest.

Tears well up in my eyes at his bravery. I feel so proud of him.

'I used my full firepower and, from the walls, my brothers and sisters began to emerge. When the White Folk saw the dragons crawling out from the walls of their houses they fled in terror.' Cinaed's eyes fill with love at the thought of the hatchling dragons. 'They are so beautiful, those new-borns and the first thing they did' – If a dragon could gulp then Cinaed did now – 'They came and freed me. With their tiny claws and teeth they freed me from the web net.' He looks at us both, his eyes amazed at the thought. 'But the White Folk were watching and, when they saw what the hatchlings were doing and how defenceless they were, they grew bold – and they returned and started to slay them – and so began the battle.'

Now Cinaed is no longer the helpless creature that started this tale, his anger fuels him, he is in his power now and utters a great Dragon War Cry that has Samardashee on his feet, hand on his sword, but Cinead is engrossed in his tale, reliving the battle. His anger is replaced by excitement.

'What they did not know is that a dragon grows fastest in times of stress so that, at every attack, my brothers and sisters would grow in size and strength. Some were slain but those that survived grew stronger. The more the White Folk fought, the bigger and stronger my Dragon Warriors became.'

Cinaed throws back his head and laughs long and loud at the recollection. The laughter triggers something in Samardashee – for this is the boy who has been raised to slay dragons, taught that they are the enemy, and this is the moment that King Samardashee, son of King Qahir the Conqueror and Sheikha Esther the Warrior Queen of the Dryseas, shows himself to be the son of his parents.

The strength of the bonding with Cinaed had overridden all this – until now. The turmoil of his past conditioning and the mysterious force that is the bonding are at war within him. He starts trembling as the emotions rush through his body: fear and anger, love and passion surge through him in an instant. I see the conflict in him as this dragon laughs at creating an invincible army. All his years of training as a Dragon Slayer come into force and anger takes over.

All this time I have been translating, sometimes hesitating, trying to dilute the words as I sense Samardashee's anger but sometimes it is as if he understands everything that Cinaed is saying before I translate. And this laughter needs no translation.

Cinaed has his eyes closed as he laughs – and this is what saves him and gives King Samardashee his moment. The King leaps up and plunges his sword into the most vulnerable spot – the dragon's eye.

Cinaed roars. Fire flares from his nostrils and burns through the platform at our feet, revealing a scene of terror and destruction – for the newborn dragons are still fighting the White Folk. Those dragons that have not been able to rise to the challenge lie dead or dying before our very eyes.

There are a few dragons, grown almost to full size, whose fury is terrible to behold. They destroy the humans easily with their deadly talons and lethal fire.

This sight is what saves us – for Cinaed, with his one good eye, sees this and sees how easily his kin are destroying the humans. He turns and looks at King Samardashee with a new respect.

'You are such a puny race, so easy for us to destroy - yet you fight us. I did not understand how you could have slain my people – not until now.'

After I translate this I turn on Samardashee, 'Do you realise what he has done? He left his people in the midst of a battle to come to help you.'

Cinaed could take Samardashee down with one swipe of his talons, one blast of his fiery breath – yet he does not. He looks on Samardashee with a love and understanding that I can only wonder at and then I realise that I feel the same about both of them – I love them both and I don't want them to destroy each other. The surge of emotion fills me with surprise – I almost don't want to admit it to myself.

Then I see the tears falling from Cinaed's eyes, gold drops, hot and molten, pouring onto the ground and into the volcano shaft – and *The Handbook* opens at a new page:

The Dragon Keeper's Handbook

'When a Dragon weeps for the love of Man, his tears will be of pure gold and he will transform the world of Man and Dragon.

It will herald a time when they will live side by side in peace and harmony. The Dragon that weeps such tears will be loved and wondered at and the man that makes him weep will be the greatest King to rule on earth.'

When I stop reading I see that King Samardashee is crying too. He has his arm around the great dragon and weeps at what he has done. No words pass but the understanding between them surpasses words. Samardashee regrets his terrible action and weeps in remorse. Cinaed forgives him and this is even harder for Samardashee to bear.

He stands on the great beast's forearm and reaches up to remove his sword from Cinaed's eye.

Cinaed opens his wounded eyelid to reveal a

great black slash in the greenness of his eye – the blow has penetrated deep enough to blind him but not deep enough to kill him.

We look into the shaft and see the golden tears cascading down and the White Folk are looking up and holding out their hands, catching the pure gold tears. But they do so without avarice. They are catching the tears of forgiveness and they weep. The dragons stop fighting and are also weeping, looking up at Cinaed, their rescuer – bonded to them for life – who is now their brother, father and leader. The sun shines down and, from where I am; it looks like a crown on this magnificent dragon – Cinaed, King of the Dragons, herald of the new age.

Hatching The Dragon

Cinaed is so big now that he can carry us both on his back with ease. We fly down the shaft and, this time, I can see all the layers of different stones – diamonds, rubies, emeralds.

Below us the fighting has stopped for with the dragon's tears came a seeing – and the White Folk and the dragons can at last see that the fighting is useless.

There are three dragons left and all look to Cinaed who towers above them. Some dragons have been slain by the White Folk, their newly-hatched bodies vulnerable to the swords and spears that the White Folk carried, and many of the White Folk lie slaughtered.

The White Folk look at their dead and wounded and it

is as if the scales have fallen from their eyes. 'Why did we do this? We can live alongside the dragons. They want to nest. We want a place that is safe from the sun. It is not for ourselves we mine these stones, we only mine them to give to Vlast as payment to stay down here.'

'You can stay here if the Dragonfolk agree,' says King Samardashee to the White Folk.

Suddenly, I'm pushed from behind. It's so sudden that I cry out as I fall forward.

'What are you doing?' Samardashee asks me.

'Someone pushed me,' I tell him but there's no-one behind me.

It happens again. By now, everyone is watching me and I *know* there is no-one behind me. I take off my backpack and something is moving inside it. I open it and

384

The Handbook jumps out and opens. Everyone is waiting, expectant, so I read it out to them:

The Dragon Keeper's Handbook

'The Dragons only fight the White folk to protect the Earth. When the White Folk are too greedy by taking too many stones, this unsettles the Earth.

There should never be more than four Dragons in Set at any one time for the four corners of the Kingdom: North, South, East and West.

Samardashee looks around, counting – four dragons including Cinaed. Perfect! But *The Handbook* isn't finished with us yet.

'Magic is needed throughout the world and the Keepers of this magic are the Dragons. In times of need, Dragons were sent to help Set. Now it is time to give back. A Dragon is needed in the land of the Old Volcano.'

'You know what this means?' My hands are trembling with excitement.

'What?' asks Samardashee.

'The land of the Old Volcano is Scotland, where the Caledonian Dragons came from. This means the world isn't destroyed – it may still be out there.'

'The world was destroyed, only the Land of Set survives.' But, even as Samardashee says it, the words sound wrong, as if he's repeating a lesson that even he doesn't really believe. 'Besides, there is no way out from here.'

Cinaed snorts in disgust, 'There's always a way.'

'How?' Samardashee challenges him.

'You forget we dragons can fly.'

'And we need you all here to keep the Kingdom safe,' King Samardashee declares. 'We can't send out help when we need help ourselves.'

I try to re-open *The Handbook* but its pages remain firmly and stubbornly closed.

Samardashee is pacing up and down. 'I don't see why we need to listen to this temperamental book. We need all the dragons here if I'm to get the palace back from Vlast. It will take more than a burnt arm to destroy him.' He starts drawing a map of the palace, scratching it out in the earth.

Cinaed, in one majestic movement, puts his claw over the map and opens his wings with a sound like heaven's gates opening. The boy-King and the Dragon-King face each other. Cinaed lifts one of the slain White Folk up in one talon and puts the corpse in front of the King.

King Samardashee steps back in horror at the sight.

Cinaed turns to me, 'First we must bury the dead.'

'These are not my people,' King Samardashee says haughtily.

'They are *our* dead! We are responsible for their deaths and must honour them in death. *Then* I will go with you, young Azra, to this foreign land.'

'You are bonded to me, Dragon! Remember that!' declares King Samardashee.

Cinead turns his good eye on Samardashee. 'Bonded

does not mean I am not your equal,' Cinaed tells him. 'And remember, King Samardashee, how you gained your crown. A crown gained through death and destruction means your reign will also be fraught with it. If you wish to change that then you need magic and mystery. The dragons are my people, their purpose is to restore magic and mystery into the world and if a dragon is needed in the Old World – then I must go.'

I interrupt before this can go any further, 'You are needed here, Cinaed, to lead your people. They may have grown but they are still young and, besides, they are bonded to you.' I feel myself trembling inside as I say this. This may be the dragon whose shell I breathed fire onto but now he towers over me, fierce and majestic. 'We cannot leave Set in Vlast's hands. He will come and destroy your kind. He has done it before and he will do it again.'

A silence reigns.

I am thinking in the silence. *The Handbook* has brought me this far. I need to trust it. If it says we need to send help then we must find a way.

I survey the devastated underground city. The walls lie scattered. There is a stone at my feet. I pick it up and hold it out to Cinead.

'Did you hatch all the eggs?'

Cinead turns his regal head and looks at me with his piercing eyes; it's as if he reads my mind.

'Maybe not.'

So we set off with the four dragons, searching amongst the stone walls, examining those that are still standing first, the dragons breathing fire onto each and every stone, searching for any sign of life – a dragon egg hunt.

Our eagerness wears off after some hours doing this but I won't give up. 'Come on, there must be another egg.'

'What if there isn't?' demands Samardashee.

'There has to be.'

'Why is it so important?'

'Because if I hatch an egg and bond with the dragon, I can go to the Old World and still leave four dragons here.'

'You? Alone?' he looks sceptical.

'Yes. Me. Who else is there?'

He looks at me with a respect that hasn't been there before. We keep searching, turning the stones over one by one until, at last, there's a 'Kleeeuip!' from one of the dragons.

We dash over and there it is! She breathes on it again and we see the tiny dragon within. The shell is beginning to crack. Moving swiftly, I take my Dragon's Breath potion from my backpack.

'I want to make sure this time.'

Cinead lights the spill for me and, only slightly more confident than when I hatched his egg, I breathe onto this precious egg. We watch as the tiny dragon form is revealed inside the translucent shell, its spine and ribs clearly silhouetted. Its tiny heartbeat glows a deep, dark red, showing the strength of the source of its fire.

Everyone is gathered around – the White Folk, the dragons, Samardashee – we all watch with bated breath as, slowly, the egg starts to open. I glance up at Cinead and he nods. He opens his vast wings and ushers everyone away, leaving me alone at last.

I breathe more heat than flame onto it. Time ticks by, the sweat pouring down my face. I maintain the steady breathing. There is a silence that fills the cavern, a silent moment as if the whole world is holding its breath. My ears are singing as if a choir of angels is in my head as I take one last deep breath, the fire surges between my lips – and the egg opens!

I watch with my heart in my mouth, waiting for the dragon to emerge. As I do, I wish with all my heart that this will be the most peaceful, friendly dragon ever to be born on this earth. A little curious head peeps out and turns its eyes on me and I can't help but laugh for the cheekiest little dragon face emerges and, as its eyes meet mine, I see that they are the colour of my eyes – a deep dark brown and they, too, have gold flecks in them.

I fall instantly in love with this young creature, a feeling that my heart is overflowing and filling not just my chest but the whole world with the love that this creature stirs in me.

It hiccups and tumbles out of its shell, landing in my hand, and rests there while I feed it on pieces of shell. I'm a Dragon Mother! The thought both elates me and horrifies me. I'm sixteen. I've shouted about being an adult but to go overnight from being a child to looking after something that, within a day or two, could be two or three times as big as me is a pretty scary leap. Then I look at it in my hand and all that I can think is, 'It's magic!'

Death of the Dragon Keepers Book 2 Return of The Dragons

I'm shivering as we fly. I'm not really prepared for this. My hands are numb from clinging onto the harness and my nose is so cold I seriously begin to wonder if it might drop off. I pull my scarf up higher then I look down and, after the first few queasy moments, my heart soars – to be up here in the sky with the birds watching my homeland get smaller and smaller; this is the stuff that dreams are made of. But I'm getting carried away...

I'm Azra, by the way. Dragon Keeper by birth, which sounds grand but when you're born to something and have no say in the matter, well, then it's just something you have to deal with.

I'm travelling light, the food supplies look pitiful for a journey of who knows how long; a bare minimum of clothes to cover the wide range of climates we will pass through; a compass – much to Reggie's amusement, this is unnecessary weight she argues.

Oh, I haven't introduced you to Reggie. Her full name is Regnatha and she does have a regal air to her. She is 'my' dragon. I hatched her and, as I was the first living thing that she saw, she is bonded to me for life. It doesn't mean she does what I say; in fact, she often looks down that regal nose of hers with something halfway between contempt and humour which is how she regards the last item in my backpack: *The Dragon Keeper's Handbook.* This is the shape-shifting book that, when it feels like it, will reveal its secrets to me.

I'm trying to make light of it but I've never left my homeland before and we're setting off on a journey that I have no real idea of where I'm going or what will be at the other end so I am scared. I'm so scared that I really don't want to go – but this way we have some chance of getting the help we need. The alternative doesn't bear thinking about. Vlast and his army are ten times the size of our little underground motley crew. The only thing we have on our side is the dragons – but these are all new-born, still vulnerable in spite of the fighting that they've been through. We need help from the old dragons if there are any still alive. It's up to me to find out.

The migratory birds have spent all night arguing over how long it takes and which route is best for us to take but a lot of their information is second or third hand, along the lines of:

'I met a swift who flew from Scotland to Africa in five days.'

'Well, the Blue Teal Ducks say it takes thirty days minimum. Those swifts eat and sleep on the wing, never mind the sex!'

And there's a chorus of tweeting laughter.

Whereas Regnatha just sits there, looking imperturbable, saying, 'I'll find it.'

I know innate knowledge is wonderful but I'm still nervous and I keep hunting for *The Dragon Keeper's Handbook,* wondering what form it has hidden itself. If it decides you aren't ready for the information then it won't reveal anything to you, clamp its pages shut and even transform itself into something else entirely which is, more often than not, a large rock. It stayed in this form for years when it was hidden by my mother's grave and its magic seems to have got just plain stuck – so its attempts to change form don't quite work and it ends up half rock half whatever it is trying to turn into, or maybe it just feels safer like that.

The one thing that it has shown me is a map. It's a very sketchy map. I don't like the look of it at all but it's really all we've got to guide us on this journey out of our desert homeland, across what looks like a whole world of what the map simply calls *'Vast Ocean'*.

The only thing that I know for certain is where we

are headed – Scotland, our ancestral home. Regnatha is descended from the Green Cryptid dragons and I am one of the Mackenzie clan from the line founded by Dougie Mackenzie, the solitary Dragon Keeper who accompanied the Scottish dragons to my homeland, the Kingdom of Set.

There have been dragons in Scotland for millennia so I am hopeful they still survive and will help train our young dragons.

Regnatha is an optimist, which is great ninety per cent of the time but on a journey like this, when she keeps saying, 'We don't need a map, just trust me,' – well, if I could throttle her great scaly neck I would.

The Dragon Keeper's Handbook took Reggie's remarks as an insult and went into a sulk for three days after this, telling me that we didn't appreciate it.

It was against this trip from the very start. At first, it refused to come with us and hid itself as a shoe until it realised we were planning to go without it. So, to try to redeem itself, it then, triumphantly, produced this map – which, to be honest, is a *great* relief for me.

Of course *that* gave Regnatha the hump as she is saying her instinct should be enough.

I'm hoping these mood swings are just a symptom of being a young dragon but if I'm having trouble handling a young dragon, I don't know how I am going to handle these ancient Scottish Dragons that I'm asking a favour, a boon, a request – I still haven't worked out what I am asking for. Well, I've three thousand miles to come up with the right words.

Dragons, temperamental books, magic – how did I get mixed up in all this?

The Death of the Dragon Keepers

Characters

Aggie Jonas (nee) later Nejem – Azra's mother, Dragon Keeper.

Arwin Nejem– Azra's father, Dragon Keeper.

Azra – the Last Dragon Keeper, daughter of Dragon Keepers Arwin Nejem and Aggie Jonas.

Cinaed – meaning 'born of fire.'a.k.a. 'Stroppy'the leader of the Dragons.

Fakhr al Badiah – Samardashee's horse. Whose

name means 'Pride of the Desert.'

Granpa Silas Jonas –Aggie's parents and Azra's grandfather.

Gramma Jonas – Aggie's parents and Azra's grandmother.

Khalil Quatrough – King Qahir's great-great-grandfather, creator of the Forest of Content and the biosphere for all of Set.

King Qahir–'The Conqueror', so-called for his defeat of the Dryseas tribes and the slaying of the dragons in the Great Dragon Wars. Father of Prince Samardashee.

Lady Constance Mackenzie– assumed her middle name, her

grandmother's surname, Jonas when her father disowned her.Sister to Aggie and Azra's aunt.

Lord Pacatore–one of the key figures at Court descended from an impressive lineage of inbreeding which has resulted in this lovable buffoon of a man.

Lord Vruntled – like Lord Pacatore he is descended from an ancient and respected lineage of courtiers. Unlike Pacatore he still believes he has power at court and believes he holds a key role. He is afraid of being taken as a fool and hopes his association with Lord Pacatore provides a favourable comparison for him.

Mackenzie–the clan from which all red-haired Settlers are descended, being sired by Dougie Mackenzie the Scottish Dragon Keeper who accompanied the Caledonian dragons to Set.

Rufus the Tinker–a.k.a. Rufus the Inventor.

Prince Samardashee–a.k.a. Sam, son of King Qahir the Conqueror and Sheikha Esther.

Sheikh Abu–leader of the Al Watan Al`atshaan translated as The Nation that Thirsts, the collection of tribes who inhabit the Dryseas. Married to Sheikha Esther.

Sheikha Esther – became leader of the Dryseas tribes on

the untimely death of her husband Sheikh Abu. Later wife to King Qahir and mother of Prince Samardashee.

Syed – leader of the Church of Set.

Vlast–Chancellor, brother to King Qahir and uncle to Prince Sam.

The Seven Warriors and the Ruby Shards.

The largest ruby shard goes into Samardashee's eye.

Adib – The Wolf. The ruby shard goes into his heart.

Azi-Dhaka – the Dragon Slayer. The ruby shard lodges in his skin giving him a skin that nothing can penetrate. Like a dragon he can only be killed through the eyes or by poison. This also gives him greater insight and affinity with the Dragons.

Baligh the stutterer – afflicted with a debilitating stutter. The shard lodges in his tongue and he becomes Baligh the Eloquent.

Merilin – The Court Hunter. The ruby shard goes into her nose, sharpening sense of smell and instinct.

Murray – The Sea Warrior. The ruby shard enters his heel,

making him fleet and tireless of
foot.

Ochamore–the fiercest fighter.
The ruby shard goes into his
fighting hand.

Glossary

Acquisitor – one who has learned or acquired some of the skills of a Dragon Keeper. Not a true-born Keeper but some were reputedly as skilled as a Flamemarked Keeper.

Al Watan Al `atshaan –The Nation of Thirst

Cryptids –animals and plants whose existence is derived from anecdotal or other evidence, considered insufficient by mainstream science.

Djinn–supernatural mystical creatures; they are spirits often found in the desert and can be

of fire without smoke or
composed of dust and sand –
dust devils.

Dracoman**–**one who can
converse with dragons in
Draco, the Dragon tongue. A
dracoman is born with the skill,
a *dragoman* can learn it. After
the Dragon Wars the term
became an insult and meant
someone with a serpent's
tongue, not to be trusted.

Dragoman –see Dracoman.

Dragon's Breath**–**a technique
of fire breathing thought to
emulate a dragon's fire
breathing.

Dragonflyers**–**officially they
were called cyclopters. Using

wings hewn from slain dragons, painted in an attempt to hide their origins, but everyone knew they were dragon wings. These were attached to the cyclopter–a complicated system of pulleys and wheels that were operated by the pilot. The pilots were the fittest athletes in the kingdom and they needed all their strength to power these complicated machines.

Dragon Keeper–only a true Dragon Keeper is born with innate magical powers. Only they can access the The Dragon Keeper's Handbook and speak Draco intuitively. A true Dragon Keeper is born with a flame-shaped scar on their body. It is often inherited but not necessarily passed on. The

passing of the Dragon Flame
from father or mother to son or
daughter is almost as
mysterious as the art of dragon
keeping itself.

Dryseas – the desert lands that
surround the kingdom of Set
so-called as they stretch like an
endless sea.

Erg–a sand dune in the desert.

***Flamemark or Dragon
Flame***–a flame-shaped
birthmark that is the sign of one
singled out as a Dragon Keeper

Greek fire–a mysterious
invention used as an incendiary
weapon whose ingredients are
still veiled in secrecy, used by
the Byzantines especially in

naval battles which meant fire
could burn on water, also
known as sea fire or war fire.

keffiyah–a traditional
headdress worn by desert tribes
as it provides protection from
the desert heat

oud–Agarwood or oud is the
rarest most expensive wood on
the planet. Its rich, woody
perfume comes from the
agarwood tree when they are
more than 100 years old. More
highly prized and valued than
gold.
Constance uses it as an aid to
meditation and for mental
clarity it is renowned for love
and is used in magic formulas
to draw a lover near.

Setdamn–a term of abuse used particularly against Settlers.

Sinsterine–a term of abuse, for someone thought to be cursed, unlucky. Corruption of the Latin 'sinister'.

Sunbox–a cooking device powered by the sun's energy

tinker–one who mends pots pans and metalwork, a dangerous occupation after the ban on fire

White Folk – the people who dwell within the volcano, distinguished by their white, almost translucent, appearance and sensitivity to sunlight.

Thanks

So very many people have helped this book on its journey and I thank them all whole-heartedly. An especial thanks to Jane Noble Knight for her inspiration and introduction to the invaluable and patient Sian-Elin; Deborah Hadfield for her friendship and belief, Pat Smart and Lou Gerring for being there, Michael and Mishka Barnett for their spiritual support and Black Forest influence! Ken Hay for his great questions and encouragement and willingness to meet over long cups of coffee! Tarimo for introducing me to the Caledonian Dragons and Hal Bishop for his Arabic tips. And last but not least, Sue Taylor, Heather Murdoch and Jayne Goldstone for encouraging this into book form.

28856002R00247

Printed in Poland
by Amazon Fulfillment
Poland Sp. z o.o., Wrocław